"Kiss me, Marly. If you don't feel anything, then I'll walk right out of here."

Marly stared at Jack. For her sanity, she really wanted him to walk away. The problem was that she knew she was going to feel something— already did as he approached her with calm certainty.

Jack reached her within three steps and caught her chin in his hands, angling his head over hers.

No, I'm not doing this. But then she was. His lips touched hers and a hot streak of lightning hit her in the gut. Her nerve endings tingled and sent a deep shiver of pleasure along her spine. He dropped his hands to her waist and hauled her against him so that her breasts flattened against the wall of his chest.

A kiss? This was no ordinary average kiss.

This was a full-on sensual assault.

Blaze™

Dear Reader,

As an author, the ultimate behind-the-scenes person, I am often fascinated by other people who work backstage, so to speak.

When I sat down to write Marly's story I had just seen a television feature on hairstylists who cater to celebrities. How much pressure it must be to cut the hair of a VIP! Especially one who's on camera all the time. One slip with the scissors or razor and millions of people will see the mistake.

Then I started to wonder what it would be like to *date* the VIP—especially if he was from a completely different background and perspective. And so along came Jack, the hero of *Midnight Madness,* in his Gulfstream jet and chauffeured limousines. And Marly, far from being impressed, won't give him the time of day because he seems like such a "player."

I had fun reversing the power between the governor and his hairstylist! I hope you'll enjoy reading Marly and Jack's story as much as I did writing it. Let me know—I love to hear from readers c/o Harlequin Enterprises Ltd., 225 Duncan Mill Road, Don Mills, Ontario M3B 3K9, Canada. And visit my Web site at www.KarenKendall.com.

Enjoy!

Karen Kendall

KAREN KENDALL
Midnight Madness

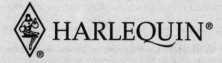

HARLEQUIN®

TORONTO • NEW YORK • LONDON
AMSTERDAM • PARIS • SYDNEY • HAMBURG
STOCKHOLM • ATHENS • TOKYO • MILAN • MADRID
PRAGUE • WARSAW • BUDAPEST • AUCKLAND

ISBN 0-373-79256-5

MIDNIGHT MADNESS

This edition published by arrangement with Harlequin Books S.A.

® and TM are trademarks of the publisher. Trademarks indicated with ® are registered in the United States Patent and Trademark Office, the Canadian Trade Marks Office and in other countries.

www.eHarlequin.com

Printed in U.S.A.

ABOUT THE AUTHOR

Karen Kendall is the author of many disasters and twelve romantic comedies. Still shuddering at the memory of those at-home, bowl-over-the-head haircuts by Mom, she thinks that good salon professionals are worth their weight in gold—and twenty times their weight in chocolate!

Books by Karen Kendall

HARLEQUIN BLAZE

Don't miss any of our special offers. Write to us at the following address for information on our newest releases.

Harlequin Reader Service
U.S.: 3010 Walden Ave., P.O. Box 1325, Buffalo, NY 14269
Canadian: P.O. Box 609, Fort Erie, Ont. L2A 5X3

For Shear Geniuses Mando, Danielle,
Carmen & Donna and last but not least Faye.
Thanks to all of you for sharing your stories and keeping
my hair out of my eyes, over my ears and highlighted
to cover the (shhh!) emerging gray.
Love you guys!
Karen

1

CUTTING THE GOVERNOR'S hair is no different from cutting any other man's—it's just that if I slip with the scissors, the result could be on national television.

Marly Fine sat awkwardly in the stretch limo, her black nylon bag balanced on her lap. Outside the windows, LeJeune was a parking lot. The heavy Miami traffic crawled alongside the long white car; people on their way to work just like she was. Heat shimmered up off the pavement, mixing with exhaust fumes and humidity and general impatience. The combination steamed the outside of almost every automobile's windows while the occupants hid in their air conditioning.

In a lime-green Beetle on the left, a college girl munched on a cereal bar and bobbed her head to the radio. To the right, a black Volvo eased forward, its driver a heavy-set Latino businessman reading the *Herald.* Behind him, a well-endowed platinum blonde in a silver Mercedes applied her brakes and half a tube of mascara at the same time.

Marly's palms sweated and she resisted the urge to

wipe them on her long cotton gypsy skirt. Examining her blue toenail polish, she wondered again if she should have changed it to pink last night.

No! She got annoyed at herself for even thinking it. *I am who I am. If the Gov doesn't like blue polish or sequined rubber flip-flops, then that's his problem. I'm only there to cut his hair.*

John Hammersmith, aka The Hammer, might be Florida's JFK reincarnated, but that didn't mean she had to wear a pillbox hat, pumps and a suit to meet the man.

"Temperature comfortable, miss?" asked the chauffeur, whose name was Mike. The poor guy actually wore livery—complete with cap—in this heat.

Marly started to nod, but her teeth were almost chattering. "Actually, Mike, can we warm it up a little back here?"

"Sure thing."

"Thanks." She wore double tank tops over her gypsy skirt, but they did little to keep her warm in the blasting air conditioning.

Marly hugged her bag as if it were a teddy bear and told herself she wasn't nervous. Hadn't *Shore* magazine named her as one of the top five hairstylists in the Miami area? Wasn't she having to turn away clients now, or pass them on to Nicky, her flamboyant coworker? In fact, she could have referred The Hammer to Nicky, except that she was afraid of the consequences.

All they needed at After Hours Salon and Day Spa was a very public lawsuit against one of their employees—for groping The Hammer's…uh, hammer. And it was an all-too-likely scenario: not only did Nicky wear tight orange spandex, but he waxed eloquent on the horrors of underwear and the beauties of copping a good feel.

She and Mike exchanged chitchat as the limo purred along in the sweltering heat, bringing her ever closer to the hair follicles of Florida's forty-fourth fearless leader. A man whose politics made her cringe, and who awoke deep feelings of resentment within her. He had the same slick demeanor of old Patrick Compton, the state representative from her hometown.

The Pattywhacker, they'd called him. He'd won office on promises of honor and sincerity and devotion. Funny how all those had gone out the window when he'd hooked up with the big boys in the House.

Didn't people ever learn? Now the good citizens of Florida had fallen for this young turk with the conservative agenda and soulful blue power ties that matched his wide-set eyes. The guy had charm in spades, plenty of hair and the big white teeth necessary for the perfect photo op. He'd promised to restore order, morality and conscience to Florida—as if the last two could be legislated.

Marly's mouth twisted and she leaned her head back, resting it against the fat braid of dark hair that hung to midspine. The plush leather seat hugged her body, and she wished suddenly that her dad was here beside her, taking a ride in a fancy limo. She'd have to tell him all about it when she visited.

The temperature inside the car had just warmed when

they pulled up under the curved portico of the Mandarin Oriental hotel, where the chauffeur got out and opened her door. Marly slid over on the seat, gave him her hand and stuck first one foot and then the other out the door and onto the pavement. Her silver toe ring flashed in the sun, as did all the sequins sewn onto her rubber flip-flops.

Mike murmured something to a bellman, who produced a cell phone and led her inside while he hit a number on speed dial. He nodded at her. "Miss Turlington, the governor's assistant, will be down for you momentarily."

Marly nodded, slung her bag over her left shoulder and put a hand up to her braid, just to make sure her hair wasn't working its way out of its confines. She licked her suddenly dry lips and shifted her weight from one foot to the other.

She moved her attention to a massive floral arrangement in the center of a table in the lobby, discovering upon close inspection that the flowers were rubber and plastic. She'd begun wondering how, exactly, a factory created these things and how many cancer-causing fumes the workers inhaled during the process, when a no-nonsense older woman in a gray suit approached her from the elevators.

Maria Turlington introduced herself with a gaze as cool and dry as the hand she proffered, and fixated for half a second longer than was polite on Marly's blue toenails. "If you'll follow me, Miss Fine, the governor will see you now."

Ms. Turlington reminded Marly strongly of someone, and as she got into the elevator behind her she tried
to think of who it was. Her hair was short and graying,
and she had a figure like a broomstick. The gray suit
was relieved only by single pearls in her ears and an
old-fashioned circle pin on her lapel. She looked as if
she lived on tea and cucumber sandwiches or something as equally bland and proper. And the woman's
shoes were positively hideous. Though they were good
quality leather, they were squat penny loafers elevated
only about an inch by a chunky square heel, and Ms.
Turlington wore them with suntan-colored panty hose.

Marly decided that anyone who still wore suntan-
colored panty hose could *suck* on her blue toenails.

The elevator stopped at the top of the building and
the two of them exited, passing a couple of plainclothed
bodyguards. One of them took a look into Marly's bag
before letting them into the governor's suite.

She shrugged as he pulled out three pairs of long,
wicked-looking scissors and an electric shaver. "Tools
of the trade." She couldn't very well cut The Hammer's
hair without them, could she?

But maybe she should write in to *Alias* and suggest
an episode where Sydney Bristow assassinated a bad
guy by pretending to be a hairstylist. Who knew?
Maybe they'd already done one.

The bodyguard frowned at the scissors and her, and
exchanged a glance with Ms. Turlington, as if to ask
whether she'd vetted Marly's background. Ms. T.
nodded, and he let them go. *Great, the FBI has a file*

on my finesse with long layers. They know about the woman whose hair I turned purple back in beauty school, and they've looked into the dangers of me giving Hammersmith a mullet with neon-green hair extensions....

They knocked and then entered an elegant suite dotted with arrangements of flowers that had once actually grown somewhere. At one end of the room, near a window overlooking the ocean, was a desk and a rolling leather chair, turned away from them. Resting against the back of the chair was a head covered by unruly, dark curly hair.

"I need you to modify that paragraph in the Orlando speech," Hammersmith said into a cell phone. "I am not saying that. Yeah. Thanks, Ricky. Gotta go." The governor spun around in the chair and stood, his eyes riveting on Marly's face.

The last thing she'd expected was for the man to be half-naked! His chest was broad, exceptionally well-defined and lightly furred in the morning sunlight.

She felt her pleasant expression freeze in surprise and her tongue instantly absorb all the saliva in her mouth. *That* was what those white button-downs and blue silk ties covered? She'd imagined a doughy, career politician's torso, well-padded with complacency and pork—not this ripped expanse of hard muscle and tanned, very masculine flesh.

"Governor Hammersmith, may I present Miss Fine?" said his assistant. "And," she added with asperity, "may I get you your undershirt, sir?" She said the word *sir* as if she meant "small, naughty boy."

Marly bit back a smile. Suddenly she knew who Ms. Turlington reminded her of: Miss Hathaway from the old "Beverly Hillbillies" show.

"Miss Fine," said The Hammer, striding forward and taking her hand, "this is a definite pleasure." He looked deep into her eyes and blinded her with a potent smile.

God help me, thought Marly. *He's twenty times more magnetic in person than he is on television.* She had to avert her gaze or start babbling incoherently. So she dropped her gaze to his chest again.

"Thank you for coming all the way over here just to cut my hair."

Nipples. I'm staring at the governor's nipples. There's something deeply wrong with this scenario. "Um, you're welcome. Thank you for asking me."

Hammersmith seemed just as taken with her chest as she was with his, truth be told. She could almost feel his eyes searching for the bra straps that weren't there under her double tank tops. She could almost feel his gaze spanning her waist, too, and evaluating the length of her legs under the gypsy skirt. She resisted the urge to wiggle her toes as he looked at those.

"I've never seen blue toenail polish," he said.

He had to be kidding. What century did he live in?

"It's the same color as your eyes."

She forced a smile to her lips. "I think that's a compliment…."

He nodded. "What do you call that color of blue? Royal? Cerulean?"

"Rebel," she said with a self-conscious shrug. "That's what the manufacturer calls it, anyway."

"Rebel," he repeated, his eyes scanning every curve of her again. "I like it."

Ms. Hathaway—uh, Turlington—bustled back in with a plain white T-shirt and handed it to Hammersmith with a meaningful glance. He nodded his thanks at her and dropped it on the desk. Then he sat next to it and gestured Marly toward the rolling chair.

Ms. Turlington's lips thinned in disapproval and she resembled nothing so much as a skinny, bad-tempered owl in pearl earrings.

"Was there something you needed, Maria?" the governor asked innocently.

"Your shoes and socks are near the sofa, *sir*."

"Why, so they are! Thank you for calling my attention to them. Now, maybe we could all have some coffee from room service?" He turned toward Marly. "You like coffee?"

She shook her head. "Chai or green tea, actually. Thanks."

"Will you order all of that, then, Maria?"

"Right away, Governor. Have you had breakfast?"

He shook his head and suddenly his blue eyes gleamed. "You know what sounds good? Strawberry waffles with syrup and whipped cream. You like waffles, Miss Fine?"

"Yes, but no, thanks."

"Whole grain toast, fruit and a boiled egg is what your nutritionist has on the menu for you, *sir*."

The Hammer waved a dismissive hand at his assistant. "That guy is a puritan and a sadist. Get me the waffles, please. And an extra-large orange juice."

"But the carbohydrates—"

"—are delicious. Thanks, Maria. Be sure to order yourself something. I'll let you know if we need anything else." And the governor slung an arm around her stiff, thin shoulders and walked her to the door. "What would I do without you, hmm?"

"I'm sure I don't know, sir." And Ms. Turlington, the poor dear, exited with as near to a flounce as she was capable of.

"She thinks she's my nanny," The Hammer said.

"Mmm." Marly was noncommittal. "So...what would you like to do with your hair?"

"Well, I was thinking along the lines of Billy Idol or Dennis Rodman."

She choked. Governor Hammersmith wasn't at all what she'd expected.

"I figured that look would go over well next time I had to speak to a Rotary Club or cut the ribbon at the grand opening of a new senior citizens home."

"So you'd like me to pierce your ears, too—and custom order a spiked dog collar? Rip the sleeves out of your Brooks Brothers' button-downs? And how about a few tattoos?"

"Exactly." He nodded. They exchanged a look of amused understanding. Then he ruined it. "You're even prettier than the picture in *Shore* magazine."

She felt her cheeks warming as she opened her nylon

bag and pulled out a salon cape. Not only should she cover that chest for her peace of mind, but also to protect him from the little hairs that would fly everywhere during his haircut.

"I said to Maria, 'She's really cute. Call that one.'"

Marly lifted an eyebrow. *Great way to pick a stylist, Governor. What if I'm a really cute butcher?* But she didn't say it out loud. "What happened to your regular hairdresser?"

"She just had a baby," he explained. "And she's retiring for a while to be a mom. I didn't have time to look for someone else in Tallahassee before this meeting, so we called you."

She was back to looking at his chest again, and all that male skin and muscle was having a bad effect on her. Her breathing had gone shallow and heat had bloomed at the back of her neck, under her arms and in other places she didn't want to think about.

"Are you Irish?" he asked.

She blinked, then shook her head. "Dutch by heritage."

"All that dark hair and the big blue eyes and the flawless skin—I thought maybe Black Irish. Though you're not pale—your skin's sort of olive."

"There's some Greek back there somewhere," Marly said. "And you? You have the same coloring."

"English, though my great-great-grandfather married an Italian. They say I get my looks from her."

Marly found herself wanting to touch his skin, just run a hand over those shoulders and those biceps. She hadn't had this kind of visceral reaction to a man since college. He put every nerve and ion in her body on full alert. *Get a grip, stupid. Why do you think they call the guy The Hammer? Apart from his surname, he nails a lot of women.*

John Hammersmith was a world-class flirt, and he'd been seen and photographed with all kinds of jet-set beauties. There'd been the Colombian emerald heiress, the Yugoslavian model, the English industrialist's daughter, the Parisian countess, the New York fashion editor and the famous, double-jointed fitness instructor. The list went on and on. The Hammer's personal little black book was reputed to contain ten volumes, or something like that.

It was a wonder there weren't dozens of little illegitimate Jacks running around, but rumor had it that The Hammer owned stock in Trojan. Recently, however, she'd heard rumblings that his handlers wanted to marry him off. It was hard for a playboy to be taken seriously in politics, especially when his platform preached morality and conscience.

Hypocrite. Marly scowled and dug for her scissors.

"What's that look for?" the governor asked. "You have something against Italians?"

"Huh? Oh…no, not at all. I was thinking about something else." Too late, she realized how rude that sounded.

He grinned that thousand-watt grin at her, and parts of her body she was unaware she had melted. Oh, yuck. Was she really that susceptible—and to a Republican?

"Do I bore you, Miss Fine?"

"No…I'm sorry, I've just been distracted lately." She scrambled and came up with a bit of truth to try to salvage things. "Until yesterday, I was afraid we were going to lose our retail space at After Hours and have to default on our business loans. It was scary. But everything's okay now."

It helped when the landlord was crazy in love with your business partner. She wouldn't be surprised if Troy and Peggy ran off to Vegas and got married, in fact.

"I'm glad to hear it. I couldn't have my favorite hairstylist going out of business—even temporarily."

Marly's eyebrows pulled together and she forced herself, once again, to look away from the man's chest. "How can I possibly be your favorite hairstylist when I haven't even cut your hair yet, Governor?"

"It's a mystery, isn't it?" He looked intently into her eyes again and she felt more exposed than if she were naked. Marly shifted her weight from foot to foot.

"Do you believe in love at first sight, Miss Fine?"

She gripped her scissors tightly and backed away from him. No matter how good-looking and charismatic and half-naked, the guy was starting to exasperate her. And what a cheesy line! "No, I do not."

He sighed. "I was afraid of that. And I have a feeling it's going to take a lot of effort to change your mind."

2

LOVE AT FIRST SIGHT? Marly couldn't help herself. She rolled her eyes. "Come on, Governor. You can do better than *that.*"

He crossed his arms over his delectable chest and actually had the gall to look offended. "You think that's just a bad come-on."

"I certainly don't think it's a good one!" *Great, Marly. You couldn't have played along, dodged the pinch to your ass, and added John Hammersmith's name to the After Hours' client roster? What's wrong with you?*

"So you wouldn't believe me if I told you that the moment I saw your picture in the magazine, I knew you were The One?"

Marly gaped at him and was saved from having to answer by the arrival of room service and Ms. Turlington again. Marly poured herself some green tea and watched The Hammer drown his strawberry waffles in syrup and smother them with whipped cream, for all the world like a little kid. A demented little kid…a Republican one. Ugh.

Really, she should leave now, while there was someone else in the room to act as a buffer.

"Did you know that my great-great-grandmother was essentially a mail-order bride?" Hammersmith said around a mouthful of waffles. "The Italian one."

"No." Marly took a sip of her tea and tugged on her braid, which had grown tight. Her scalp prickled with discomfort and something like alarm.

"Great-great-gramps saw a cameo portrait of her, and that was it for him. He went to find her and bring her back to the States."

The tiny hairs on the back of her neck jumped to attention. Then they parted to make way for a deep shiver. But she didn't react visibly, just eyed him with a tolerance reserved for the insane.

"Isn't that romantic?" the governor said, swallowing. He ate standing up, his plate in his left hand, sawing through the waffles with the edge of his fork.

She nodded for Ms. Turlington's benefit. Marly might not have finished college, but how stupid did the man think she was? He figured he could feed her this pack of BS and she'd tumble into bed with him?

It was a lowering thought that she might have done so based on the recommendation of his bare chest alone. She could have just had a fling—to support morality and conscience and Republican values, of course. But there was no way she'd do it now, with this lame talk of love at first sight. How many women had he snowed with this stuff?

Ms. Turlington changed the subject, bless her bossy,

crabby, proper little heart. "*Mister* Governor," she announced, eyeing his plate with something like despair, "you'll note that there is an egg-white omelet under that steel dome. Those waffles you're consuming—with the entire udder of butter and bathtub of syrup—contain a minimum of 3,600 calories and—"

"Turls, you know I detest egg-white omelets, and you probably had them fill it with broccoli and onion, too."

"—six hundred grams of carbohydrates, not to mention enough saturated fat to deep-fry a herd of buffalo."

"But I do thank you for your continued concern about my health. It's very sweet of you."

Miss Turlington sniffed. Then she produced a bona fide white, lacy handkerchief and dabbed at her eyes.

"Turls…" the governor groaned. He cast her a look of long-suffering, set down his waffles on a stack of scary-looking legal documents sporting lots of little yellow flags and plucked the steel dome off the omelet plate.

Ms. Turlington stopped dabbing immediately and looked hopeful.

Marly thought the omelet looked and smelled fabulous, but the Hammer wrinkled his statesman-like nose. He poked at the mass of eggs with a knife and looked unimpressed. He set the dome back over the plate, and just then Marly's stomach had the poor timing to growl. She hadn't eaten anything before leaving her apartment.

He brightened. "You're hungry!"

"No, no," Marly stammered, under Ms. Turlington's ominous gaze.

"Yes, you are. Isn't it fortunate that we ordered some extra breakfast!" The gov grabbed a fork, cut a bite of omelet and made choo-choo noises, driving it toward her mouth.

Marly was so appalled that she opened it and he deposited the bite of eggs onto her tongue, emitting a long engineer's whistle as he did so. Then the lunatic said, "Yum, yum!" and sent her a big ole shit-eating grin.

She almost spat the eggs onto the carpet at Ms. Turlington's expression, but she managed not to. Instead she swallowed them.

"Now," said the Hammer, advancing on her with a napkin, "you just be a good kid and eat the omelet. I'll return to my breakfast of champions. Turls, where's your oatmeal and prune juice?"

"I have already consumed my morning meal," growled Ms. Turlington, and swept from the room, closing the French doors with a snap.

Marly blinked. "Governor, really, I'm only here to cut your hair." She looked at her watch. "And I've got to get back. I have a client coming at ten…."

"It'll take you all of five minutes to eat that omelet, sweetheart. C'mon, can't you do it for the Ham?" He advanced toward her and put his hand at the small of her back.

His touch was casually intimate, for someone who'd just met her. Though she thought he was nuts, her body didn't agree. Marly leaped forward as if burned and grabbed the plate of eggs. She held it in front of her like a shield and dodged around the serving cart. "Thanks."

"Can't have you all shaky when you're snipping the gubernatorial locks, eh?" He grinned. "Gubernatorial—isn't that the weirdest word? Sounds like all things relating to a goober."

Marly laughed in spite of herself.

"Now, my family and friends know the truth—I am one, but do we need to advertise the fact?"

He didn't look at all like a goober. He looked like blue-blooded sin in half of a thousand-dollar suit. And he was crazy. Obviously. Because he insisted on returning to their earlier topic of conversation.

"Now that I've found you, Marly Fine, I'm going to have to insist that we get to know each other. Are you free for dinner?"

Marly set down the omelet once again. "No, Governor, I'm not. We run a salon, which is open until midnight."

"You work a sixteen-hour day?"

"Sometimes. Usually I work a twelve-hour one. I go in at noon. Miami is half-Latin, and Latins like to keep late hours."

"Hmm. I'm asleep by eleven. This could be tough to work out…." He stuck another bite of waffle into his mouth.

Her sense of outrage rose. "Governor Hammersmith, while I am certainly, um, flattered by your interest, there is nothing to work out. I have a very full life and—"

"You married?"

"What? No."

"Engaged?"

"No, but—"

"Boyfriend?"

She hesitated a split second too long.

"Then we can work something out."

"Governor, maybe I don't want to *work something out!*"

"I've been told I'm passably handsome. I floss regularly and use mouthwash. I can even be charming, when I want to be." He cocked his head to one side and licked a bit of whipped cream out of the corner of his mouth. "What's not to like?"

Marly closed her eyes. Then she opened them and took a deep breath. "Women don't say no to you very often, do they?"

He looked a little sheepish. Then he shook his head.

"In fact, I'll offer a guess that not many *people* say no to you."

Hammersmith stuck the last bite of waffle into his mouth and chewed pensively. Then he shook his head again.

"Well," Marly said brightly. "We all encounter new experiences, don't we? Now give me that—" she took the plate from his hand and set it on the cart "—and come sit down in that rolling chair again so I can do my job."

He blinked at her, then went and sat down. She unfolded the salon drape and threw it around him, covering him from the neck down. *Thank God I don't have to look at that chest any longer.*

Then she handed him a mirror. "Now, you like a side part on the left, correct?"

He nodded.

"And it looks like…are you having these strands near your temples *colored* gray?"

"Yes. They decided I looked more statesman-like with a little silver around the edges."

Marly pursed her lips. "I don't have anything with me to do color. All I can do today is a cut."

"Isn't that a shame. Guess you'll have to see me again, won't you?" His lips twitched.

"You know," said Marly severely, "if you were anyone but the governor, and if you were even a smidgen uglier, I wouldn't put up with you."

"Even though you're curious?"

"Who said I was curious?"

"Your eyes, your voice, your body language. The fact that you're still here and haven't run screaming out the door—even though you think I'm crazy."

She glared at him. "I don't *think* you're nuts. I *know* you're nuts."

"We'll see about that. History often repeats itself."

Again, a shiver spiraled around her spine before dispersing into hundreds of tiny ions of unease. Marly dug her spray bottle of water out of her nylon bag and depressed the nozzle several times, soaking the man's head.

"I guess that's one way of telling me I'm all wet," said The Hammer. "But by the way, if we're going to ride into the sunset together one day, you should call me Jack."

3

RIDE INTO THE SUNSET together?

"So you see," Marly said later to her business partner Alejandro, "the guy is off his gubernatorial rocker!"

They stood on the salon side of After Hours, on the zebra floor cloth and in front of a tangerine wall. The spa was funky and colorful, with Italian glass lamps, walls of all colors and a distressed concrete floor painted to look like the ocean. Every time she looked at it, Marly felt a mixture of pride and horror: *she* had painted it, crawling around on her hands and knees to do every lovely little blue-green swirl. Ugh. She had, in fact, driven the design of the whole place, since she'd studied art during her three years of college and had a knack for interior design.

Alejandro stretched his six-foot-four, muscular frame. A yawn overwhelmed his classically handsome face. He rubbed the day-old bristle on his square chin and sipped at a beer, his treat for passing his business school exams and squaring the books. "Oh, I don't know, *mi corazón*. If I didn't think of you as a sister, *I* might fall into instant love with you."

"Be serious!"

"I am." He rubbed absently at an uncharacteristic stain on his elegant linen pants.

Shrieks of drunken feminine laughter rolled over them, coming from the pedicure stations in the back. Marly lifted an eyebrow. "Let me guess, the Fabulous Four are here? Aren't they early?"

The Fabulous Four was a group of women in their forties who booked their appointments together each week and got blind drunk on After Hours' wine. At first Marly had thought it was cute. But after an entire year, it was getting a little out of hand. The Fab Four took over the place and got so loud and raunchy that sometimes other clients complained.

"They're all going on a cruise together tomorrow," Alejandro explained. "So they moved their pedicures—and happy hour—back to lunchtime."

"Did they fight over you, honey?" Alejandro was often in demand for hand and foot treatments, as much as he hated to give them.

"No—when I found out they were coming, I deliberately crossed myself off the book for that time slot." He grinned. "Now, tell me more about the governor."

Marly frowned. "He's feeding me lines, and I'm not going to fall for them. How many times a week do you think he tells the story of his great-great-grandfather and the mail-order bride?"

"*I'll* go to bed with him," her coworker and fellow stylist, Nicky, said with a leer. "He's hot…for a Republican. Yeow, baby! I'd leave nothing on the guv but one of those royal-blue neckties…."

Marly shook her head at him. "I don't think he's bent your way, Nicky-doll. And I didn't get the feeling he'd care much for orange spandex, either."

"Oh, *gawd.*" Nicky shook his blond hair. He was like Princess Di in drag, with a California accent and a lisp. "It's back to the Internet for me, then. Did I tell you about my date last week? Finally, *finally,* I thought, *yay,* this guy is gonna be *it.* He was *good*-looking, head to toe Calvin *Klein,* makes tons of money as a designer. *I was ready to marry him*—Even though we'd have to go to Massachusetts to do it! And then he shows up wearing those plastic *food-service gloves.* He wouldn't even take them off to shake my hand! Fuh-reak, freak, *freak.*"

"But, Nicky," said Alejandro. "You wouldn't know what to do if you had a normal date. You'd have no stories to tell us and nothing to complain about."

"So true," said Nicky with a frown. "Do you think I should see a shrink about this?" He wandered off, one hand on his spandex-encased hip.

Marly sighed. "He makes the governor seem normal, honestly."

Alejandro laughed. "Don't you mean *Jack?*"

"I'm not going to call him by his first name. And besides, even if I was dumb enough to fall for his lines, how can I ignore the fact that he's been seen all over the state with that debutante…you know, the one they're expecting him to marry, like, yesterday?"

"Carol Hilliard?"

"Yeah—the one in the pastel Chanel suits and the Ferragamo shoes."

"Nobody's seen a rock on her finger, Marly."

"They're probably still excavating it, all hundred carats, from Daddy's diamond mine."

"Meow!" Alejandro winked at her. "What has she ever done to you?"

"Nothing," muttered Marly. "She's just perfect for him and I'm not. Do you know the guy had never even seen blue toenail polish before? I guess it's not fashionable among the little debbies."

"Marly, *chica*. Why does it bother you that you're not perfect for him?"

"It doesn't."

"Right. That would be why you're obsessing."

"I'm not obsessing! I was just sharing my morning with you. A morning that happened to include a half-naked governor who's a big flirt."

"Ooooh, is he cut?" Nicky was back again.

"Um, well, yeah."

"Six-pack?"

She nodded.

"On a scale of one to ten, how much chest hair?"

"Five."

"Mmm. Sounds divine. You should sleep with him." And with that little bit of advice, Nicky disappeared to mix color for his next client.

"He hasn't asked me!" she called after him, hands on her hips. Not that Jack Hammersmith needed to, really. She knew exactly what it meant when her body got that boneless feeling, the melted knees syndrome, the warm rushes of sensation in private areas.

"So," Alejandro said. "You cut his hair. And you're not sworn to secrecy, so that's great PR for After Hours. The best, in fact. The only thing better would be for us to cut the hair of Brad Pitt or Colin Farrell. Would you get to work on that, please?" He grinned.

She heard his unspoken request. *Don't piss off the governor. We can use the cachet and the extra clients he'll bring us.*

Alejandro owned the biggest percentage of the spa and therefore owed the most money on the business loans they'd taken out. He constantly worried over finances, even though he masked the concern with his Latin charm.

She and Peggy had never told him how close they'd come to being kicked out of the retail space. He would have flunked all his business school exams or something. To reassure him, Marly said, "Hammersmith's coming in here in a couple of days so I can do his color. I'll have to use a private room, though—he doesn't want to advertise the fact that he gets gray highlights to make him look older and more experienced. Isn't that funny?"

Alejandro shrugged. "What is he, thirty-six or so?"

"Something like that."

"You can understand it—most of the guys he's working with in the Florida state legislature are on the far side of middle age, and he needs their respect."

"Uh-huh." Marly yawned. "I wish I was going to get out of here before midnight…."

"I'm sorry, *mi corazón.* Tell you what, dinner's on me later. We'll order from Benito's. Sound good?"

"Thanks. You're a sweetie. But what sounds good is a three-week vacation in the Caribbean. I've got to start limiting my schedule, Alejandro. I can't keep going like this…. I haven't been to see my parents in months, and as for spare time…" Spare time was a dream. And forget spare time to paint.

"I know. Give it a little longer? Then we'll bring in a couple more hairdressers, and everyone can ease up on their appointments a bit."

Marly nodded. "You know I don't mean to belly-ache, hon. I've got my dad's medical bills, but you're under even more stress, with the whole business school thing."

She only had a few more months to go to pay off the thoroughly scary multithousand-dollar hospital bill that she'd had sent to her, because if her father had seen it he would have relapsed, gone into renal failure and died.

She'd worked a deal with the administrator: only a quarter of the bill balance was sent to her parents. She'd dropped out of art school and begun working immediately to pay it off, since they were on a fixed income.

The pace of her work these days was killing her, but she focused on the light at the end of the tunnel, when the balance would be paid.

What would it be like to have spare time again? A social life? She couldn't wait. Marly went to greet her next customer and initiated the normal chitchat while she snipped and reshaped the woman's hair.

The rest of the day flew by: she cut the hair of a city

council member, wove blond extensions in for a local model, did a short, spiky style for a woman who owned a boutique around the corner. She snipped, textured, shaved, highlighted, gelled, moussed and sprayed. Then she did it all over again.

By 10:00 p.m. her feet were throbbing and she was exhausted—but they had two hours of prime party time to go. Marly looked longingly at the wine Shirlie, their receptionist, brought to the customers, thinking that just one glass would do a lot to ease her pain and give her a second wind.

But it was an extremely bad idea to cut someone's hair under the influence...so she'd wait and have her wine after they'd locked up.

She welcomed her 11:00 p.m. client, Regina Santos, and sent her off to be shampooed. Marly's thoughts turned renegade again, toward Jack Hammersmith, his bare chest and his mouthful of waffles. The way his tongue had licked the whipped cream from the corner of his mouth. The way he'd looked into her eyes as if he could see into her mind, and his calm certainty that she was The One.

The One what? The one who'd tell him that the Hammer wasn't going to nail her?

JACK HAMMERSMITH successfully dodged Turl's urges to take an extra vitamin and got dressed in front of the maid whom Housekeeping sent to remove his room service cart. He gave the maid credit for waiting until he put on his shirt and tie before she asked shyly if she could take a picture of him with her camera-phone.

He said, "Sure, sweetheart—do you want a photo of us both?" Turls pressed her lips together and did the honors, before almost chasing the poor woman out.

Jack would much rather have signed two dozen autographs or taken as many photos with hotel staff than get down to work with Stephen Lyons and Jorge Martinez, his top aide and his campaign manager, respectively.

But they barged in at 9:45 a.m. regardless of his personal preferences, and worse, they forced him to crack open the thick manila file folder on the suite's desk. They pulled out three of the yellow-flagged documents and handed him a pen snagged from behind Martinez's ear.

"Do you wash those ears?" Jack teased him, pretending to wipe earwax off the pen. "Because I know you've always got one or the other of them pressed to the ground, spying and dragging them in the dirt."

Martinez shot him a cool glance. "That's why you pay me the big bucks."

Lyons started yakking at him about pending legislation in the Florida state senate. When he paused for breath, Martinez jumped in. "I've hired a professional PR firm just to manage your press coverage—and consult on your image—during the campaign."

"Great, more people to push me around," Jack said in jovial tones. "Well, I'm sure they'll approve of my haircut. You like it, Lyons? Marty?"

They stopped talking at looked at his hair. "It's great, Jack," said Martinez, and moved on to a new topic: the train wreck that a public school initiative had become. Lyons made a circle out of his thumb and forefinger, spreading his other three fingers wide in the A-Okay sign.

"Hey, Lyons? Your wife—does she ever wear blue nail polish?"

"What? No. Twelve-year-olds and rock stars wear blue nail polish."

"And artists, wouldn't you say? Creative spirits."

"Jack, can I get you to focus, here?" Lyons asked.

"I'm very focused," said The Hammer.

"Oh, Christ," said Martinez. "What inappropriate woman are you obsessing about now?"

"She's not inappropriate. She's perfect."

"Jack, if she wears blue nail polish, she is not perfect. I have one name for you—Hilliard. She's beautiful, she's connected, she's got style and wit and fashion sense. You've known her all your life. Now will you please, for God's sake, get engaged to the woman? It could make or break your reelection campaign."

"That's crazy. It's not my prospective wife who's running! I got elected single last time. Why is it so important that I be coupled now?"

Martinez sighed and sat in a club chair. He spread his knees and dangled his clasped hands between them. Not a hair on his head fell forward, however; it was all sprayed into place.

"The polls, Jack. People cut you some slack before because of the way Lady Annabel dumped you so publicly."

"I dumped her!"

"A matter of spin, Jack. Poor Hammer, left practically at the altar…"

"I would never have married her!"

"Water under the bridge, Jack. The point is, now the polls are reflecting that people think you're too wild. They don't want a playboy running the state—they want a responsible, settled adult. They'd love to see little Jacks bouncing around the capitol lawn."

"I fail to see how that's anyone's business but mine."

"Jack. Don't be naive. You're a public figure with a political career at stake. You could be in the running for a vice-presidential seat in the next six years or so. Get your ass married to an appropriate woman or jeopardize all that. Do you hear me?"

"Loud and clear, Martinez." Jack cast him a glance of impatience, bordering on dislike. The waffles sat heavy in his stomach and the syrup and whipped cream gurgled. He should have eaten the damned whole-grain toast and omelet, but he was beyond sick of being told what to do every second of every minute of every friggin' day. Leader of the state? Hell, he felt more like a trained ape.

Jack, who'd grown up in politics like his father before him, found it hard to take it all seriously. Politics wasn't his calling; it was Dad's calling, but he'd found himself fresh out of law school and going into retired Senator John Hammersmith's law firm, without even an interview. His experience was so alien compared to that of his friends, who clerked and schmoozed and interviewed wildly—everywhere from Miami to New York to San Francisco.

He'd felt guilty and not particularly deserving of his golden-boy status as John Hammersmith Jr. born with a pedigree and dimples to match.

His mother had a law degree and connections, as well. But if she wanted to, she had the luxury of fading into the woodwork and just being exceptionally well-married. Jack wondered what it was like to have options like that; be female; choose your role in society.

Did she feel guilty about not being more of a trail-blazer? Had she burned her bra back in the seventies, only to walk right back into its harness like an obedient broodmare? He mused about it. Jeanne kept her mouth shut about such things.

Martinez was waxing poetic about poll numbers and Lyons advocating that he play in some charity golf tournament.

Jack nodded, the waffles in his stomach gurgled around some more, and he found himself thinking about Marly Fine. He put a hand up to his neck, still feeling her cool, efficient hands in his hair and the rhythmic snipping, eyes always measuring, gauging length and proportion and thickness.

He had a lot of hair. If he ever let it grow, he'd probably resemble an afghan that had just stuck its paw into an electrical outlet.

Marly had done an exceptional job of making him look suave and *goober*natorial. But suddenly Jack wished he had rock star hair and maybe an earring through his nose; a different perspective on life and how to live it. A perspective that would make him more appealing to a woman who wore blue toenail polish and no bra and a long gypsy skirt that Jeanne Hammersmith probably wouldn't give to the housekeeper for polishing the silver.

He hadn't lied when he'd said that the instant he'd seen her picture he'd known Marly was The One. He'd seen it in her cool blue-green eyes and the dark sheen of her hair. In the way she held herself and the tilt of her pointed little chin.

She was the kind of woman who inspired love songs. She was a Helen...a woman who caused men to do crazy things. Such as tell her within moments of meeting her that she was The One.

Jack grinned. Because she hadn't giggled and blushed; she hadn't taken it as a come-on that could help her career if she played ball. She'd just told him flat-out that he was nuts.

The general public didn't tell Jack that he was nuts—only his inner circle did. So Marly had stepped into that circle without even trying.

The public treated him with deference and respect that he wasn't convinced he deserved. Then there was his father, who didn't respect him much at all—but who envied him.

"I didn't have anybody's coattails to ride when I got elected senator," he was fond of saying—especially when he'd had a couple glasses of Basil Hayden's finest bourbon. "I did it on my own steam."

Yeah, well, some of us have more steam—aka hot air—inside us than others, Senior.

Rock star hair. Yup, that's what he needed for the re-election campaign. And maybe a sapphire nose ring instead of the blue silk power ties. He'd appeal to the younger demographic, create an identity for himself apart from the Hammersmith name.

Jack blew out a cynical breath. *Yeah, right. And I'm gonna grow a breast on my forehead, too.*

Because he was stuck with the Hammersmith name—and even worse, he was Hammersmith *Junior.* Chip off the old blockhead.

He tried to focus on what Martinez and Lyons were droning on about now, but he had a hard time caring. Instead he wondered exactly what his great-great-grandfather had said first to the Italian girl he'd crossed continents to find.

Had he said, "*Signorina bellissima,* I know you are The One?" Or had he actually employed some subtlety? Jack had never found subtlety particularly useful. Either people didn't catch it at all or your message was diluted entirely.

Subtlety was not to be confused with the fine arts of political innuendo and favor-currying. Now he excelled at those…but wasn't exactly proud of the fact.

Yeah, the more he thought about it, he needed to cultivate rock star hair and maybe one of those terrible little soul patches on his chin. That sure as hell would appeal to the conservative voters—about as much as a girlfriend who wore a long braid down her back and no bra.

No bra…hmm. The Hammer suddenly wondered if Marly had a policy against underwear altogether. He really wouldn't mind finding out.

4

"So?" SHIRLIE, the receptionist at After Hours, nudged Marly the next day. Her pale blue eyes sparkled with curiosity and every spiky, mascara-covered eyelash jutted forward eagerly, like antennae wired to collect information.

"So, what?" Marly looked through a stack of pink message slips for any calls that needed to be returned before the evening. Misty Horowitz, Sandra Tagliatore, Janine Burbank. No—she could call all of them later.

"The governor!" Shirlie kept probing. "What's he like in person? Is he as hot as he is on TV?"

"Hotter. Though he's going to develop a belly to rival Buddha's if he keeps on eating the way he eats."

"What does he eat? Is he nice?"

Marly laughed. "He eats little boy food—waffles and syrup and whipped cream."

"So was he nice or did he treat you like the hired help?"

"He was…very affable." *Besides being crazy and trying to use a bad line to get me into bed. Who does he think he is?*

"So what's his body like? It's hard to tell under those suits."

"Nothing wrong with the man's bod," Marly said before she could censor herself. "He greeted me without a shirt or shoes."

"No!"

"Yup."

"How big are his feet?"

Marly sighed. "You know, your obsession with penis size is really not healthy, Shirl. How many times did you try to find out the number of inches Troy Barrington sports?"

Shirlie didn't bother to blush. "I'm taking a survey for scientific purposes."

"Right. And my grandfather was a prima ballerina."

"So I'll give you the goods on T.B. if you tell me The Hammer's foot size."

Marly rolled her eyes. "That's a myth, the foot size thing."

"It's not! Research shows—"

"Whose research? Let me tell you, the shortest guy I ever slept with, the one with the smallest feet, by the way, had the most gargantuan schlong."

Shirlie's eyes widened. Then she thought about it. "Well, Troy has giant feet, judging by his shoes, but Peggy told me he's hung like a piece of elbow macaroni. This blows all my survey results out of the water."

Marly poked her tongue into her cheek. "Did Peg tell you that when she was angry? Because I don't buy it."

"Ohh." Shirl stuck the eraser end of her pencil into her ear. "I didn't think about *thaaaat.*"

Be careful, hon, or you'll shove it right out the other

side. Marly grimaced at herself. She shouldn't be so bitchy—Shirlie was a great receptionist and all the customers loved her. They hadn't hired her because she had a Ph.D.

"I've got to get ready for my next appointment, Shirl. Just give me a buzz when she shows, okay?"

"Yeah," said Shirlie, frowning in concentration, the pencil still in her ear. "So does the Hammer have toe hair? Because that can be a factor, too."

Don't poke your eye out with that, little girl. The pencil obviously wasn't tangling with a lot of brain matter.

"Toe hair?" said Marly. "Uh, I really couldn't say."

She went to the back of the salon, removed her scissors from the black nylon bag and stowed it away in a cabinet. Then she went to her station and started straightening things. She gazed fondly at the photo of her dad she kept there; acknowledged a tinge of guilt that she didn't have a picture of Mom there, too. She sprayed the mirror with Mountain Berry Windex and wiped it clean. She stared at her makeup-free face and wondered just what it was that Jack Hammersmith thought he'd seen in it to feed her that cheesy line. Gullibility? Naiveté? General lack of intelligence?

Okay, so there was a hidden romantic part of her that thrilled to the story of his great-great-grandfather and his Italian bride. But there was also a big part of her that said, hey—even if it's a true story—the woman saw an opportunity to marry a rich American and have herself a bit of freedom and adventure in a

whole new world. She could have just been an opportunist who didn't want to marry the village shoemaker
or butcher. By no means was it sure that she'd fallen
in love....

"Oh, *gawd*," said Nicky behind her, into his cell
phone. "He wanted me to turn vegetarian for him! *Yes!*
Can you believe it?"

Marly tried not to listen to what Nicky was talking
about. The last time she'd overheard one of his private
conversations, she'd found out more than she wanted
to know about the possibilities of chest hair transplants.
Imagine a guy having hair-plugs on his chest.

"Get out!" Nicky shrieked.

She winced.

"I don't believe it." He ran a hand through his *sun-
streaked* golden locks. "You're telling me. This Internet
stuff is for the dogs...except dogs are luckier. They just
run up to each other and sniff each other's butts."

Okay, I just do not want to hear this phone call. Marly
headed to the kitchenette for some green tea, shaking her
head. Nicky was definitely the most flamboyant gay man
she'd ever met. The others she knew were a little more
subtle, a little more restrained in their demeanor. Nicky
was a neon gay pride banner with a built-in squawk box.

Speaking of squawks...that sure sounded like
Shirlie up front. Had a cockroach crawled in the door?
Marly went up front out of curiosity, remembering too
late that it had killed the cat.

Governor Jack Hammersmith smiled at her from
the doorway while behind him, two bodyguards—or

secret service or whatever they were—scanned After Hours for thugs, terrorists or kidnappers.

One of them honed in on Nicky's orange spandex pants. The other one honed in on Shirlie's twenty-two-year-old breasts.

Marly gaped at The Hammer. "What—are you doing here?"

"I thought I'd just stop by to see if you had time to—"

"I'm all booked up," said Marly. "Sorry."

"Actually," said the ever-helpful Shirlie, "you had a cancellation at two, and, as you can see, Deirdre is more than ten minutes late, so you could take him now."

"Fabulous," said the governor with a smile that would have had Mother Teresa on her back within ten seconds. He stuck out his hand. "I don't believe we've met. I'm Jack."

"I know who you are!" gushed Shirlie. "Ohmigod, you're twenty-times-better-looking-than-on-television! Sometimes the makeup's too heavy and the color's off and they make you look orange, know what I mean? And close-up shots with that gooky powder can be *soooo* gross, right? Anyway, I'm Shirlie! Welcome to After Hours, the salon and day spa!"

"Er, thank you, Shirlie," said Jack.

"So do you like public speaking, or does it bother you? I just hate public speaking." Shirlie babbled. "My palms sweat and I shake and I always wonder if I have lipstick on my teeth or mascara smeared under my eyes or my bra strap is hanging out. You?"

"Well, I don't have those particular, uh, issues, but I do know what you mean."

"Ohh! I wasn't trying to say you're a drag queen or anything, you know? I mean, that would be pretty funny, The Hammer with his bra strap hanging out, ha, ha, ha!"

"Ha," agreed Jack, politely. He cast an alarmed look at Marly.

"Did someone say drag queen?" Nicky skipped up.

"No." Marly was emphatic.

"I could have sworn someone said it!"

"Governor, if you'll follow me into one of the spa treatment rooms, we'll use that so you have privacy." She shot him a tight smile and put her hand on his shoulder to steer him back there. The two secret service apes lunged forward, one with his hand in his jacket.

Her eyes wide, Marly said, "I specialize in color, not assassination or recreational kidnapping."

They didn't crack a smile, but The Hammer did. "It's okay, boys. I tried to tell you, that really was art camp she attended in her junior year of high school—not an Al Qaeda training program. All she can do is draw me."

Dear God. They really *had* done a background check—a thorough one. They knew about… Suddenly furious, she said in clipped tones, "Wouldn't I have murdered him yesterday morning, boys, scissors to the jugular, if I had such festive plans?"

She turned on her heel and marched away, wishing that her rubber flip-flops would bang across the floor instead of whisper silently.

"Temper, temper," Nicky murmured before she was out of earshot.

"Ohmigod," said Shirlie. "She is so, so, kidding around. I mean, she's not violent. I heard her be really rude to a telemarketer once, but honestly, that doesn't count. They call at the worst possible times, don't you think? And they're so pushy."

"Yes," Jack said. "I think I'll just…go get my color done, now. Thanks."

Marly heard his wingtips clip-clopping across the cement floor, walking on her painted water. And then he was in the doorway, his eyes on her face. The security detail had followed, of course. "Can we leave Frick and Frack outside for a moment?" she asked.

Jack turned his head. "Frick? Frack? Do you mind?" Then he stepped inside and shut the door behind him.

"I'm sensing a definite hostility here," he said. "Should I have called for an appointment?"

"Yes," said Marly. "But that's not the point. The point is that I didn't give you permission to dig into my background. It makes me angry and uncomfortable."

He nodded. "I'm sorry. It's just SOP, I'm afraid. Standard operating procedure."

"Why? I didn't come asking for the job—you picked my face out of a magazine! And now those goons probably know the first boy I kissed and the brand of my underwear."

He opened his mouth to say something and then apparently thought better of it. "Would you rather I left, Marly? The last thing I want is to make you angry."

The governor is apologizing to me. Me, Marly Fine, hairdresser. How weird is this?

She gave a fierce yank to her braid and then tossed it behind her shoulder. "No. I don't want you to leave." Alejandro would kill her. And…she was curious. She might as well admit it. There was a certain level of intrigue to this situation.

"Good. Because I really don't want to." Jack smiled that drawer-dropping smile of his. She could feel his sex appeal tugging at her own drawers. God, the guy could be president one day, elected by a vast turnout of howling women in heat.

"Would it make it up to you at all if I told you the first girl *I* kissed, or the brand of *my* underwear?"

She made a sound of exasperation.

"Her name was Teresa Miller, and we were twelve. And it's Neiman Marcus."

Great. *I really needed to know that he wears designer—*

"Boxers, by the way."

—*boxers.* She held up a hand, palm out. "Too much information."

She pulled over a hard plastic chair from the corner, and patted the seat of it. "Sit."

"I can't roll over, instead?" But he did as she asked.

"Do you want to stay gray near the temples or go more silvery?"

"Silver sounds great."

"Okay. Then I'm going to go and get the supplies I need to mix the color for you. Can you keep Frick and

Frack under control while I do that? I've never poisoned anyone by hair follicle yet—still practicing."

He grinned.

She opened the door, said, "Don't shoot," and walked right past the goons. Their expressions were as deadpan as those of the Queen's Guard. All they needed were some tall dead animals on their heads like their British counterparts and they were good to go.

She mixed her color in a plastic bowl and took it, with a paintbrush, back to the room where she'd stashed the governor. They squinted at the bowl of gook suspiciously.

"Would you like to test it for explosives?" Marly asked. "Sniff it? It smells really nice."

Frick exchanged a glance with Frack that probably meant, in security-detail speak, that he'd love to crush her windpipe so she couldn't mouth off anymore. She flashed him a lovely smile and shut the door again in their faces.

"Did you paint the mural in this room?" The Hammer asked. "It's great. Very…whimsical."

Marly nodded. "Thanks."

"You have an art degree?"

"No." She let the word lie there, unadorned and bald. She wasn't about to explain about dropping out of college after her junior year to help pay her father's medical bills. She'd dragged him to an endocrinologist not covered by the welfare program, and it was thanks to that he was alive today. But oh, God, the bills…five months to go until she was at a zero balance with the hospital. Just a short five months.

She really had no regrets. She had her dad, and as Ma had pointed out—not too gently—she couldn't have made a living as an artist anyway. So here she was, hairdresser and accused martyr. Her dad hated the fact that she was in debt on his account—of course he'd found out. Ma said she deserved it, interfering like she had and thinking she knew better than the doc at the VA hospital. Always thinking she was smarter than everyone.

Great, Ma—Marly had said, to her shame—*then when you get sick, you can rot in the VA. You can be a social security number taking up a bed, aware that the administrative staff just wants you to die so they can give that bed to somebody else.*

Marly had no idea why she could never do anything right for her mother. Was it because her parents had waited ten years to have a child and she had drastically changed the dynamic of their marriage? She couldn't answer that question, and she'd never wanted to put her father in the position of having to answer it.

The Hammer brought her back to the present. "You're a really talented artist, you know."

"Thank you." She sectioned a piece of his hair, slid a piece of foil under it and painted it with the smelly color from her bowl. Then she folded it up and secured it while she went on to another section.

"Ever want to paint canvases or furniture full time, instead of hair?"

"I love what I do, Governor." And it was true—she did. But had she ever dreamed of more free time to paint? Of course.

"Please," he said, "call me Jack."

Oh, right. Because I'm The One. "Okay, Jack. So now that you've read an entire dossier on my life and times, why don't you share some of your history with me?"

"Good point. Where would you like me to start?"

The governor now had little foil wings at each of his temples, which unfortunately didn't diminish his sex appeal. They just made him look like some kind of goofy—but hot—space alien. She tried not to laugh.

"What's your secret dream?" she asked him.

"To be a rock star," he said promptly. "Can't you see me with head-banger hair and tattoos on my chest and maybe some KISS makeup?"

He *would* have to bring up the subject of his chest again. "No."

"Not even a little bit?"

She shook her head. "Sorry."

"You're crushing me, here. Absolutely crushing me."

"Governor—Jack—you're so Republican that you squeak." And he was, judging by his looks alone. However, now that she thought about it, his actions toward her hadn't been very conservative at all.

"I've never squeaked in my life." Jack straightened and she remembered the breadth of his chest and the corded muscle of his arms. "And what do my politics have to do with anything?" He looked offended.

She cleared her throat. "Well, it's just that…I think most rock stars vote for the other side." *And then there's me—I didn't even make it to the polls during the last election.* She wasn't proud of that.

"You're stereotyping."

She shrugged. Maybe she was.

"You're trying to tell me that because of my politics, I'm not allowed to dream about being a rock star? That makes no sense at all."

"Yes it does," she insisted. "Rock is all about rebellion and anger and doing what feels good—calling bullshit on the establishment. You *are* the establishment! You're up there in Tallahassee trying to legislate morality, which by the way is never going to work…."

"You know," he said calmly, "I don't think you have the faintest idea of what I do in Tallahassee. I don't think you have a clue what a Republican is, and I know you don't understand my personal agenda."

Marly swallowed, set down her color bowl and brush on a table, and folded her arms. "Oh, really? What is it?"

Jack poked his tongue into his cheek and cocked his head at her. "In one sentence or less, I'm for streamlining big government, sweeping educational reform and the restructuring of our tax system. Does that sound evil to you?"

"Depends on the specifics." But inwardly she was cynical. *Streamlining big government* was Republican code for "throwing out all social programs" and *the restructuring of our tax system* clearly meant "giving breaks to the rich while worsening the financial situation of the poor and middle class." She only just refrained from curling her lip.

"Well, if you had about three days to listen, I'd explain it all to you. Now, what other crazy ideas do you have about Republicans? That we're all religious nuts and right-leaning and only have sex in the missionary position—solely for reproductive purposes?"

"No—"

"Because I can assure you that none of those things are true of me—and especially not the last one."

His blue gaze bored into her and all of a sudden Marly found herself remembering that the man *did* have a little hair on his toes. *Hmm, wonder if Shirlie's right about that toe hair/size connection?*

How was it possible for the blasted man to look sexy with foil wings on his head? Nobody looked good in foil. Except for him! He was in the most emasculated position possible—at least with clothes on—and yet he vibrated with testosterone. He wore it like a tailor-made suit.

It was lowering to have to place herself on a level with Nicky and Shirlie, but the shoe fit: Marly wondered with sudden intensity what Jack Hammersmith looked like completely naked, and whether there was truth in advertising. Rock Hudson was gay, she reminded herself. She unstuck her tongue from the roof of her mouth. "Governor, would you like something to drink while we're waiting?" The color had to stay in for a few minutes longer.

"Jack," he said again. "And that would be great. Just water, please."

"Will Frick and Frack need to test it for toxins or killer microbes?"

"You tell them that if they stick their tongues into my drink, they'll be guarding the mail room next week."

"I'd be delighted." Marly left the room, slipping again through the twin slabs of muscle outside the door. They didn't so much as blink at her.

Peggy, After Hours' massage therapist and third owner, was humming in the kitchen. "Hi, sweetie."

"You're humming again," said Marly, oddly touched. She hadn't seen Peggy this happy in forever. She was definitely in love.

"Oh. Sorry. Am I getting any more musical? Probably not." She grinned. "So do you really have Jack Hammersmith back there for color? I saw the limo and the security detail."

Marly nodded. "Yeah, those are hard to miss. Can you believe it? This is great PR for us."

"Just watch out," Peg warned her. "I hear the guy is relentless when it comes to good-looking women."

Marly shrugged. "He's already tried—I'll give you the juicy details later."

Peg rolled her eyes. "I can't wait. Hey, Troy and I have a couple of spare tickets to the Dolphins' game. You want to come?"

Marly would rather be thrown naked into a bed of fire ants than attend a football game. "Thanks so much, but I'm off to visit my da—uh, parents. You should ask Shirlie."

Peggy frowned. "Well, I think she still has a thing for Troy."

"I have two words for you—elbow and macaroni. Remember?"

Peggy froze and then started laughing. "Oh, God. I

forgot about that. I was furious at him, and she kept pushing."

"Well, I think she's over him, because she's now trying to estimate the size of the governor's package."

"My sympathies!"

"Yeah, thanks."

Marly returned to the treatment room with two glasses of ice water, and when the muscle heads squinted at them she repeated what Jack had said. Again they exchanged glances silently and let her by.

"Frick and Frack really don't like the idea of the mail room," she reported.

He grinned and accepted the water with thanks. They each sipped, eyeing each other warily, and then she announced that it was time to rinse the solution from his hair.

"This isn't a regular salon sink back here, so it'll be a little odd," she told him. "But come on over." She pulled the little squares of foil off and then had him bend forward. She put his head under the faucet and shampooed his hair thoroughly, while strange psychological currents eddied around them. He smelled just as good as he had yesterday morning, a little muskier because the day had worn on. The scent was a combination of soap, deodorant and a curiously citrusy fragrance—heady, refreshing and expensive. She wondered if it was a custom blend.

It felt distinctly weird to be running her fingers over this man's scalp, massaging it, when he'd said the things he'd said to her. The forced proximity to someone she wanted to keep her distance from was uncomfortable.

Nevertheless, she did her job, keeping the shampoo out of his eyes and working it in and out of his hair twice before conditioning it.

The guy even looked handsome upside down, whereas most people looked ridiculous with their jowls jostling their eyelids.

Finally, finally, she was done, and she wound a towel around his head. Usually a shampoo girl would have done all this, but they were, after all, trying to protect his privacy.

She sat him back down in the chair, removed the towel and combed his hair neatly into a side part. She reached for a blow-dryer, but he put his hand on her arm. "No, thanks. I don't want it all fluffy and sprayed into place like plastic."

"Okay. Then—I guess we're done here, as long as you like the color."

"I like it," Jack told her. "But you and I aren't done by a long shot."

She eyed him coolly, saying nothing, even though his calm arrogance irritated her.

"Will you have dinner with me?"

"Jack, I'm honored. I really am. But…let me just say that your reputation precedes you."

He got that sheepish expression on his face once again. "I know they call me The Hammer."

"Yeah. And I'm sure you have no idea why. Sorry, but I'm not up for, um, a quickie. To put it bluntly."

"I keep trying to tell you that it's not like that. Really."

She just looked at him.

"Kiss me, Marly. If you don't feel anything, then I'll walk right out of here and I won't bother you again. On the other hand, if you do—and I'm counting on you to be honest, here—then you go to dinner with me one night this week."

5

KISS HIM? Marly stared at Jack. *If you feel nothing, then I'll walk right out of here and I won't bother you again.*

The problem was that she knew she was going to feel something—already did, as he approached her with only the barest minimum of a question in his eyes. Mostly what was in them was the calm certainty of an alpha male about to take possession of something he wanted. And even though she resented being the object of that possessive gaze, a frisson of excitement flashed through her, too.

Jack reached her within three steps and caught her chin in his hands, angling his head over hers.

She closed her eyes, still thinking, *No, I'm not doing this.* But then she was. His lips touched hers and a hot streak of lightning hit her in the gut. Shocked, she half pulled away, but his hands still cupped her jaw. He looked into her eyes, slowly and deliberately, and then kissed her again, this time deeply.

Her mouth parted under his and the electricity licked at her gut again as he explored her mouth with his tongue, moved his hands into her hair and pulled it loose.

His fingers were heaven on her scalp and at the sensitive skin of her neck. Her nerve endings tingled and sent a deep shiver of pleasure along her spine. He dropped his hands to her waist and hauled her against him so that her breasts flattened against the wall of his chest.

Her nipples tautened almost painfully and heat rushed through her as Jack stroked her tongue with his own and then gently bit her lower lip. She tried to stroke his jaw, his ears—but he grabbed her wrists, pinning them behind her with one hand and backed her against the wall.

Then he devoured her again. When he raised his head and gazed down at her, the look in his eyes wasn't remotely civilized. His pupils had enlarged and his irises had gone smoky, not quite focused. His breathing shallow, he still managed to get one word out. "Damn," said The Hammer, his voice rough. "You *are* The One."

She was tempted to believe him, but it was just too easy. She opened her mouth to speak but he plundered it again, stealing her breath and whatever words had been on the tip of her tongue. He bruised her lips and licked her clean of logic or thought. He left nothing but her response to him.

And when next he raised his head, she could only stare at him. Jack stared back. Then, eyes heavy-lidded with desire, he traced one thumb over her right nipple.

If he hadn't still been holding her wrists, she might have slid boneless down the wall.

Her expression, her tiny catch of breath, must have told him all he needed to know. Because before she could even process what was happening, he had her tank tops bunched under her armpits and he'd fastened his mouth over her bare nipple.

This time her knees refused to support her and only his hand locked around her wrists and the muscular thigh he jammed between her legs held her up. She sucked in oxygen in a long, ragged breath.

Jack's tongue slid over and around the pink bud, while Marly closed her eyes and let the room fall away. Sensations rushed from her breasts to the juncture of her thighs and back again, losing her in a Bermuda Triangle of desire.

Kiss? This was no ordinary average kiss. This was a full-on sensual assault.

"You're crazy beautiful," Jack murmured, and then took her other nipple into his mouth. She sagged again onto his thigh and gave herself to pleasure.

When he raised his head and looked into her eyes again, she could only blink stupidly at him.

"Have dinner with me, Marly."

It wasn't a question, it was a command. And even though she hated being told what to do, even though she wore Rebel blue toenail polish, she nodded her head. "Okay, Jack. I'll have dinner with you."

HE WAS GREATLY relieved at her answer. His response to Marly Fine ricocheted off the charts. The way her lips yielded to his, the feel of her in his arms, the scent of her hair and the taste of her skin—in combination, it was enough to make a man lose his mind. There was something exotic and untamed about her that quickened his blood and drove him to possess her. If that was primitive and not politically correct, too bad. He literally ached to have her, to drive into that lithe, sweet body of hers.

But Jack got control over himself and straightened her clothes, even though what he wanted to do was to rip them off her and keep her naked for all time, preferably swimming in a vat of warm baby oil....

Her dark hair framed her face and hung down her back. God, he loved her hair free and flowing over her shoulders. He loved the fact that she didn't seem to wear any makeup besides a little lip gloss—which, thanks to him, wasn't there any longer. Her lips swollen and her nipples plainly visible even through two layers of fabric, she looked like a gorgeous Gypsy, one that he'd follow anywhere.

"Which evening are you free?" he asked. "Is tomorrow too soon?"

She tucked the loose tendrils of hair behind her ears and put an index finger to her lips, tracing them as he had done with his tongue. "Yes. Tomorrow *is* too soon." She was going to see her parents over the weekend. "I need some time to... How about Tuesday?"

Tuesday he was supposed to be at a charity dinner to raise money for further diabetes research. But without any hesitation Jack said, "Tuesday is perfect. Pick you up at eight?" He'd paid five hundred dollars for the privilege of being bored stiff all night. They had his money already, so should he feel guilty for feeling a stomach virus coming on? Nah.

She nodded. "Um, so…is this a double date?" She gestured at the door behind her. "I mean, will the boys be coming along?"

Jack frowned and shrugged apologetically. "It's hard for me to dodge security. But I'll tell you what, I'll make sure they're either out in the car or at a table across the restaurant, okay?"

An evil impulse sparkled in her eyes. "Would they like dates? One of them seemed impressed with Shirlie's…attributes. And we have a very cute single manicurist here, too. Or if one of them swings the other way, I'm sure our stylist Nicky would be happy to—"

His lips twitched. "Maybe next time." He looked regretfully at his watch. "I'm going to have to go—I have a speech to make to a young Republicans group."

Marly wrinkled her nose and seemed about to make a caustic comment, but he put his hand out, palm up. "Hey, I know what you're going to say. But it's better for kids to be politically active early and learn that they can make a difference. Don't you think Republicanism is better than utter apathy?"

She looked undecided at that, and Jack laughed. "I'm going to teach you the upside of conservative politics before we're through, Marly."

"Yeah? How do you know that I won't impart the wisdom of liberal thinking to you, instead?"

She looked so fierce and yet so adorably kissable. "Well," he said with caution, "I foresee a lot of spirited discussions ahead."

She pursed her lips and narrowed her eyes.

"Better not puff your mouth up like that or I'll kiss it right off," Jack told her, moving toward the door. They now both looked presentable enough to finally open it.

"You like the silver in your hair?"

He nodded. "I do. Well, as much as I can like the concept of doing anything to my hair. It's a pain in the ass and isn't exactly a manly sport. But thank you—that was a good recommendation." He hesitated. "So, will you give me your phone number before I leave?"

"I'll be here, mostly. So just call After Hours."

Interesting. She was still keeping him at arm's length, even after that kiss. She didn't want to give up any more personal information—not that he couldn't get her number through back channels quite easily if he tried. But he wanted her to give it to him herself.

"All right then," he said, trying to dismiss the kernel of disappointment. "I'll call you."

She nodded and he walked out.

He'd no sooner gotten into the car than Turls was on his case via cell phone. "Hi, Turly." Her fussy tones made him smile.

"You will recall, I'm sure, sir, that it is Miss Hilliard's birthday in two weeks."

Was it? He'd forgotten. "You're right—it *is* her birthday in two weeks."

"And I'm sure, sir, that you've already had the forethought to buy her a gift?"

She knew very well that he hadn't. "Turls," he lied, "I've been racking my brain for days, and I can't think of what to get her. I'm a guy. We're not good at this type of thing."

"Would you like me to find something for you, sir?"

"Yes, that would be fabulous—you know Carol's taste better than I do. What would I do without you, Turls?"

"I'm sure I don't know, sir. By the way, you do have Miss Hilliard's party marked on your calendar? It's coming up."

"Right. I'll be there, along with the other members of my illustrious family. Can you work with Garcia to keep Senior away from the scotch?"

"I'm not sure that we'll be successful at that, sir."

"Well, just…try. Thanks. And, Turls? I promise to eat a salad with dinner. Just for you."

ONE O'CLOCK in the morning was a terrible time to eat pizza, but they were doing it anyway, since the three of them were starved: Marly, Alejandro and Peggy. They sat at the little bleached oak table in the kitchenette of After Hours, hovered over the cardboard box from Benito's, the Italian restaurant two doors down.

Marly tipped some more red wine into the plastic cup she was using. It was a nice Australian Shiraz that blended beautifully with tomato sauce and garlic.

"Leave us some," said Peggy. "Or should I just get you a nipple to put over the neck of the bottle?"

Marly laughed weakly.

"We have another bottle in the cabinet over the refrigerator," said Alejandro. "You have as much as you want. But the price you pay is talking to your friends." He grinned at her, clearly wanting to know what was going on with Jack Hammersmith.

"Right," Peggy agreed. "You said you'd share *the details* with me later. What details?"

"The governor is in passionate pursuit of our Marly, it's clear," Alejandro told her.

He turned back to Marly. "You just cut the man's hair yesterday morning, and he 'drops by' this afternoon to see if you can see him again? Also, Shirlie informed anyone within earshot that he left a tip the size of Alaska. So you must have impressed him."

Marly tipped a healthy amount of Shiraz down her throat. "He kissed me, Alejo," she blurted, using Alejandro's nickname. "And now I have to go to dinner with him."

"What a brute!" Peggy said. "God, what if he forces you to eat fabulous hors d'oeuvres or even use a napkin? The horror!"

"Peg, be serious. I'm flipping out, here. I'm not the kind of girl who goes to dinner with the governor. I won't even know what fork to use...."

"He told her that she's The One," Alejandro said. "She thinks it's a bad come-on to get her into his bed."

"Well, he picked my photo out of *Shore* magazine," Marly clarified to Peg. "Said he knew just by seeing my face. How weird is that?"

"Hmm. Very un-Republican behavior, I have to say." Peggy looked thoughtful. "Well, do you want to go to bed with him?"

Marly choked on a mouthful of pizza, feeling her cheeks grow hot.

"Aha!" said Alejandro. "She *does*."

"So then why don't you?"

"Because…because…" Marly floundered.

"Look." Alejandro set down his slice of pizza and wiped his hands. "With The Hammer, there really is no mystery. You know he likes women. Lots of different women. So if you're attracted to him, just enjoy things for the moment, knowing that it is not serious and has no potential to be serious."

"But then he's lying to me!"

Alejandro raised an eyebrow. "Make no mistake, *mi corazón*. All men lie—especially to women. We tell you what you want to hear. 'No, that dress doesn't make you look fat.' 'Of course I like your hair that way.' 'Yes, darling, I'll love you forever.'"

"That's terrible!"

He shrugged. "It is the way of the world. There's no malice in it, really. Just take anything a man says to you with a grain of salt, and then enjoy it. We're bastards, all of us, but we have our uses. Sleep with Jack, know it's a fling and enjoy it just as a man would."

Marly swallowed some more wine. "If you weren't one of my best friends, Alejo, I really wouldn't like you right now."

He spread his hands wide and grinned. "But I am so charming and handsome."

"Kick him, Peggy—you're closer."

"Ow!"

"Take that for womankind everywhere."

He rubbed his ankle and glared at them. "Fine—next time I will not give you any insight into the male soul. You can just wonder and be mystified."

Peggy snorted. "There's no mystery to the male soul. It all boils down to four simple drives for you guys— sex, power, money and food."

"Not true!" Alejandro protested. "What about the Dalai Lama?"

"What about him?" Peg replied. "I'll bet he still enjoys food and power, at least. Besides, Jack Hammersmith is no Dalai Lama. So, Marly, I agree with Alejandro even though he is a lowly man and therefore a second-class citizen. Go forth and sleep with Governor Jack. Enjoy it. Take notes for the tell-all book you'll write later to embarrass his children. Just have fun."

Marly shoved another piece of pizza into her mouth and tried to absorb all of this practical advice. But the pie now tasted like cardboard to her. "You people are very warped," she said. "I would never write a tell-all, and I cannot sleep with a Republican!"

Peggy laughed. "Honey, if I can sleep with a football player, then you can sleep with a Republican. What is it that bothers you so much about his politics?"

"Well, for starters I come from a long line of dedicated Democrats. My dad would have a stroke if I dated someone from the Dark Side. And then there's the fact that the Republican party has always been the party of entitlement—do you know what I mean?"

"Kind of, but not really," said Peg.

"I mean that Republicans are the fat cats, the millionaires and the big-business types, and the bottom line is king to them, no matter how the little guy gets screwed. Our family has seen it in action—I told you about what happened. Because of that alone, I'll never vote Republican as long as I live."

"Fine," said Alejandro. "But you don't have to vote in this case." He grinned. "You just have to have fun."

"Yeah, I guess. Except that he has these security guys following him everywhere. What if they stand sentry at the bedposts?"

"*Eeeuuuww.*" Peg grimaced. "That does have a creep factor of nine point seven. You'll just have to get rid of them somehow."

"Well," Marly admitted, "I doubt they're right in the room, but they're definitely just outside. I don't know how Jack can live like that, knowing that his every move is watched, his every word overheard. That's another thing—if I go out to dinner with this guy, am I going to be on the front page of the *Miami Herald* the next morning?"

"I like that idea," Alejandro said. "Make sure to wear a sandwich board for your date, with our hours of operation and marketing tagline in big letters."

Marly stared at them hopelessly. "You two are *not* helping. You're not helping at all."

6

MARLY'S VISIT HOME was somewhat depressing, as usual. Her parents lived in a small three-bedroom stucco house in Fort Meyers. Little had changed since her last visit except that Dad had installed a plastic dolphin mailbox out front.

Marly got out of her second-hand Mitsubishi and braced herself to see her mother. Instead of thinking about their difficult relationship, she focused on the rip in the yellow-striped awning over her parents' bedroom window. They needed to repair that before next year's hurricane season tore the entire fixture off and blew it up into Georgia.

They needed hurricane shutters, too, since the weather had gotten so crazy lately, but those cost thousands of dollars.

Marly got her small overnight bag out of the car and hoped that her mother's vicious cat, Fuzzy, had taken up sleeping somewhere other than in the guest room. The last time she'd stayed here, Fuzzy had refused to cede the guest bed to her, and when she'd accidentally rolled over on him in the middle of the night, he'd bitten her.

She had a theory that Ma had trained the cat to attack her, using electrical shocks and the scent on her old baby blanket. There was nothing like feeling cherished in your childhood home.

She went up the cracked walkway, shuddered at the tacky wreath on the door, studded with little plastic flamingos and alligators, and rang the bell. A few moments went by before she heard heavy footsteps inside the foyer and her father opened the door, a huge smile on his face. "Hi, honey! It's so good to see you." He wrapped her in a bear hug.

He smelled the same as he always had: of Listerine and Coppertone and Dial soap. "Hi, Dad." She hugged him back, pulling away only when she saw her mother behind him in the hallway, wiping her hands on a dish towel.

"Hi, Ma." She kissed her mother's tanned, leathery cheek. "I like the new rinse you're using. That silver-blond shade is pretty."

Her mother didn't acknowledge the compliment. "Hello, Marlena. Did you have a nice trip over?" God. Only two sentences in her stiff tones and Marly felt immediately unwelcome. How did Ma do it?

Her answer was flip. "Bug count, ninety-three. Roadkill count, four. Gators seen, two."

Dad guffawed.

Ma said, "That's disgusting, Marlena. Why don't you go and wash your hands. I've been keeping the roast warm, but I expected you an hour ago."

"Ma, I told you I'd get here between five and six, not

at five…" But her mother had already disappeared into the kitchen.

Marly looked at her father, who shrugged. "Here, let me take your bag."

"That's okay, I've got it." She headed toward the guest room and stopped dead as Fuzzy raised his head and glared at her from the center of the bed.

"Yeah, well, it's fab to see you, too, you overgrown rodent." She deliberately dropped her bag next to him on the mattress, making him bounce. He hissed, obviously excited to see her. If it weren't for Dad, she'd never visit.

Marly made claws with her fingers and hissed right back at Fuzzy. He got into a crouch and growl-yowled from deep in his throat.

"In case you haven't figured this out, I'm a lot bigger," she told him. "I also travel with shears and an electric shaver, so I'd watch out if I were you. I could make you look really stupid, and none of the other cats would respect you anymore. They'd laugh at you and call you names."

Fuzzy lashed his tail and glowered at her.

"I could shave you butt-bald, leaving little poodle tufts at your feet and a Mohawk on your fat little head. How would you like that, tough guy?"

He hissed again.

She put her hands on her hips. "Let's just get one thing straight. While I am here, that is *my* bed. Not yours. Mine."

She turned and left the room to go wash her hands.

Unbelievable that her mother still directed her to do that, as if she'd remained five years old and had just come in off the jungle gym. Marly sighed.

There were new towels in the bathroom, coordinated to match the ancient avocado-hued tub. They had small palm trees machine-stitched on them and white fringe.

In the ceramic dish by the sink Marly found little soaps in the shapes of oranges and pineapples. And a green alligator candle with a party hat. *Gee, if I didn't already know I was in Florida, do you think I could guess?*

"Marlena?" Her mother popped her head in. "Use the liquid soap under the sink, and one of the old towels in the cabinet. The ones out on the bar are only for show."

Of course they are.

They sat down for dinner approximately thirty seconds after she left the bathroom. Hexagonal vinyl place mats protected the heavy oak table, and her mother had sewn plastic zippered covers for the seat cushions on the chairs.

The same Precious Moments salt and pepper shakers sat in the center of the table, along with a white angel candle whose gold wings were dissipated with cracks. The angel's halo was partially smoky and melted from the time Marly had lighted her one Christmas. She'd never heard the end of it. The angel was a *show* candle, not to be used.

Dad stood over the roast, attempting to carve it with

a buzzing electric knife from circa 1972. His hands weren't too steady anymore, and the meat looked as if it had been in the oven for about a week longer than necessary. In fact, Marly was pretty sure it had petrified.

"Dad, would you like me to do that?" she asked.

"He's fine," snapped her mother. "He's been carving the roast for thirty years now, Marlena. Why don't you pass the peas?"

Gladly. Her mother's peas came straight out of a can, after which she boiled them again and then shook dried onion and bacon bits over them, compounding the sin by adding half a shakerful of salt.

Marly had never met anyone who could punish food like Ma. No wonder she'd been such a skinny kid—she'd hated the taste of most things she encountered at the dinner table. She hadn't discovered decent cooking until she'd moved to Miami, and then a whole new world had opened up.

"Damn," said Dad, wheezing a little. "I think I'm hitting a bone, here."

"There *is* no bone in that cut of meat, Herman."

Wanna bet? The whole thing is a fossil now. Marly reached for the noodle surprise, which was Ma's moniker for bow tie pasta drowned in cream of mushroom soup, baked under a layer of plain corn flakes.

"I'm telling you, Betty Jo, I'm hitting a bone. It's either that or this thing was carved off the back end of a Cadillac, not a cow."

"I don't appreciate that statement, Herman. I don't appreciate that at all."

Dad scowled and pressed down so hard on the end of the "meat" that his knuckles went white. He kicked up the speed a level, too.

"I worked all day on that roast, and if this is the kind of thanks that I get—"

"Shi—nola!" Dad exclaimed as the electric knife suddenly gnawed through the slab of beast. The end of it went flying off the table, while the knife nicked the edge of Ma's china platter and then made a long scar in the finish.

Marly winced at her mother's enraged expression.

"What is wrong with you, old man?"

"Ain't nothin' wrong with me, Betty Jo! It's the roast. Where'd you buy it, from the lumber section at the hardware store?"

Oh, boy. Dinner was degenerating into a brawl. Marly jumped up from her seat and picked up the projectile beef from the green shag carpet. She carried it into the kitchen while her parents traded a few more insults.

She flipped on the kitchen tap and tried to rinse the carpet fibers off the meat, but they seemed to have grafted to the burned ridges. Marly knew Ma would have a goat if she threw "perfectly good food" away, but she was stymied. Finally she took the vegetable brush from the side of the sink and scrubbed vigorously, until every green hair was gone. What the hell did she do now, blow-dry the thing?

Holding it in one hand, she pulled a couple of paper towels off the roll, doubled them and set the meat on top. She didn't want to pat it dry, since the paper towel fibers would probably stick to the rough edges, too.

Her father stalked into the kitchen and glared at it. "We need something to drink with this meal. Something to wash it down."

"I heard that!" yelled Ma.

"Well, if you didn't hear it loud enough, I'll say it again." He pulled a bottle of wine out of the pantry and peered at the label. "This'll work. Peach wine, imported from Dahlonega, Georgia."

Marly probably would have drunk gasoline at this point, if she thought it would take the edge off. "Great. You open it and I'll get some wineglasses from the dining room hutch, okay?"

"Yeah." He stumped over to the utensil drawer and pulled out a corkscrew, then followed her into the other room.

Ma was slopping peas and noodle surprise onto each plate, wearing a scowl that would have frightened a crocodile.

"I like your dress, Ma," said Marly, trying to lighten the atmosphere. She got three glasses and set them on her father's end of the table.

"Don't try to butter me up."

O-kaaay. Well, then, your dress looks like you tore it off a Goodwill sofa, Ma. But Marly didn't say it out loud. It was bad enough to be rude and disrespectful in her mind.

Dad made three hefty pours out of the bottle of peach wine and set them down at each place setting with a snap.

Without speaking, Ma went around the whole table and moved them onto the vinyl place mats. Dad tightened his mouth and went back to the roast after inhaling half his glass of wine. He finally managed to carve off three pieces, and they smothered it in jarred gravy.

Marly took a sip of the peach wine and almost gagged at the sweetness of it. She was used to dry whites like Chardonnay and light, crisp ones like Pinot Grigio. Still, it was better than nothing in this poisonous atmosphere.

They got through the meal with Ma completely silent; she and Dad made all the conversation. Marly told him about funny clients they'd had, and her limo ride and how she'd cut the governor's hair. She told them she thought Peggy and Troy were on the verge of getting engaged.

Dad told her about how something was eating his tomatoes before he could get them off the vine, and that he'd caught a nice-size peacock bass last time he'd gone fishing. He worried about what was going to happen with social security.

Ma cleared the plates, waving away Marly's offer of help, and brought in individual orange Jell-O desserts embedded with raisins and chunks of canned pineapple. She'd piped Cool Whip around the edges.

"Those look beautiful, Ma."

"Not fancy enough for you, I'm sure."

"Ma! I said they look nice. I know they'll taste great, too." Marly picked up her spoon, eager to get the meal over with. They ate dessert in total silence.

When everyone was done, she insisted that her mother go and relax while she did the dishes. She scooped up all the little glass parfait dishes and spoons and fled to the kitchen.

She put all the food away, rinsed the plates and other things, then loaded the dishwasher and started it. Only then did she realize that something was missing from the kitchen counter: the projectile piece of roast.

Dad and Ma didn't have a dog. There was only one possible culprit. With a beetled brow and her hands on her hips, Marly searched the house. Fuzzy wasn't in the formal living room, the study, the back hallway or her parents' bedroom. She stalked to the half-open door of the guest bedroom and kicked it open. She saw the discarded paper towels on the carpet first, as a low growl greeted her.

Fuzzy and the piece of roast were in the middle of her bed.

MARLY DROVE back home doubting that her relationship with her mother—or Fuzzy—would ever improve. Not that she gave a rat's ass about Fuzzy. She put them both out of her mind, cranked on some loud rock and thought about a different kind of hot beef in her bed.

Tuesday night seemed to take a long time arriving, and when it did she had a hard time choosing her clothes, since she was uncertain of where Jack Hammersmith would take her.

Finally she settled on a deep ruby-red sarong and a black silk tank top that tapered to a V on one side.

She didn't own a single pair of closed-toe shoes that weren't for the gym, and she hated high heels, so she put on another pair of flat thong sandals, these in leather instead of rubber. She added dangly silver earrings and a silver cuff to the outfit and piled her hair on top of her head.

She refused to smear foundation on her face, no matter what the occasion, but she did put on mascara and tinted her lips deep red.

Marly surveyed the result in her bathroom mirror and decided she didn't look half bad. Of course, the governor was probably used to women who put on a full face of makeup and teetered around in skyscraper heels—but she wasn't going to pretend to be someone she was not.

She looked down at her still-blue toenail polish and reflected that it didn't work at all with what she was wearing. She still had ten minutes or so before Jack was due to pick her up, so she slipped off her shoes and sat on her bathroom floor to make a change.

When her doorbell rang a few minutes later, she sported silver polish—with one red rose on her left big toe. *Wonder what he'll think of that?*

She still couldn't believe she was going out on a date with the governor. The Republican governor. What if his politics were infectious and she caught the disease?

What if they argued over social programs and she stabbed him with her dinner fork? What if Frick and Frack did a flying belly-flop into the appetizers to prevent her from doing so?

Marly had a feeling it was going to be an interesting evening. But she opened the door and smiled. "Hi, Jack."

7

SHE'S IMPOSSIBLY beautiful, Jack thought, drinking in the sight of her. She'd done something to her eyes to make them even more exotic and mysterious, and her lips looked like cherry-flavored sin.

Though her fingernails were short and bare, she'd painted her toes silver, which he found highly erotic. Silver with one suggestive, carnal-red rose. And—was she trying to make him spontaneously combust?

Because that skirt was really no different from a tablecloth knotted at her waist, perfect for a picnic in a secluded spot on the beach.

Marly didn't smell of any overpowering, commercial perfume. She wasn't hung with jewelry like a human Christmas tree. And she didn't tinkle with artificial laughter.

She didn't make him wait half an hour while she finished getting ready—in fact, she didn't invite him in at all. She said, "Let me get my bag," and left him standing in the doorway.

But Jack was curious. He wanted to see her personal space. So he stepped inside and looked around. The apartment itself was…very apartment-like. What Marly had done with it, however, was simply amazing. The walls were draped in exotic fabrics and giant floor pillows dotted the carpet, which she'd mostly covered with a gorgeous Oriental rug. Little jeweled lanterns hung everywhere, along with paintings and intriguing collages. And candles dotted every available surface.

She'd created a colorful, exotic bazaar, and Jack loved it, despite the fact that it was utterly foreign to him. That was part of its charm.

"Marly, this is fantastic!" he said as she came out of the bedroom with a little embroidered tapestry handbag.

She flushed with pleasure. "My friend Peggy says I'm going to set the apartment on fire with all these candles. But I'm actually very careful." She walked to the window and pulled the filmy drapes aside. "Isn't the view gorgeous?"

Jack raised an eyebrow. She overlooked some kind of hideous factory complex. "Uh…"

"It's why I took the place. I pay extra for that view." She laughed and let the drapes fall back into place. They obscured the factory in a romantic, feminine haze. "So, are you ready? Where are we going?"

I'm ready to throw you down right here on your Oriental rug. But Jack tried to remain civilized, even if he felt anything but. He ran a finger around the suddenly too tight collar of his shirt. "Where are we going? It's a surprise."

He put a hand to the small of her back and felt her

quiver. Christ, just anticipating having her was going to kill him. He wanted to do a lot more than make her quiver.

Jack wanted her crying out, begging for release and thrashing in ecstasy.

But he felt ashamed by his desire, because she was a whole lot more than a hot body who triggered an animal reaction in him. Marly Fine was complex and delicate and soulful—but strong. How many twenty-year-old girls would drop out of their dream art program—one for which they'd received a full scholarship—to shoulder a parent's crippling medical bills?

Again, Jack wasn't proud of having read the file on her, but he hadn't been able to help himself. And he was stunned at her sheer strength of character.

He waited while she locked her apartment door and took her elbow as they walked down the stairs. The limo sat gobbling gas at the curb, garnering curious stares from residents on their way in and out of the building.

Marly seemed embarrassed by it, and he wished he'd brought a normal car instead. But he'd wanted to give her the full treatment, so to speak. Now he realized that she wasn't the sort of woman who was impressed by the trappings of his world.

Mike, his personal chauffeur, saw them and hopped out of the driver's seat to hand them into the back.

"Hi," said Marly. "How are you?"

"I'm fine, thank you, miss. Governor, Mr. Lyons is trying to reach you. He says you're not answering your cell phone."

"Correct. Whatever it is can wait."

Marly looked at him as she settled herself onto the seat. "You don't think—I mean, I don't mind. It sounds as if it's important."

Great. He'd been trying to assure her that they'd have quality time together, but now she thought he was neglecting his duties to the state. "All right. Thanks." He dug the damn phone out of his pocket and hit the speed dial. "Lyons?"

While he listened to his advisor foam at the mouth over what he deemed a crucial poll on how the Florida voters viewed him, Marly began a conversation with Mike.

"So, do you have children?" she asked him.

"Sure do, miss. Ages two and four, girl and boy. They're a handful." He laughed good-naturedly.

"Are they home during the week, or do they go to day care?"

"Day care's name is Grandma Eulala, which is lucky for us in a lot of ways…but unlucky in others."

She looked a question at him.

"I get to do all her remodeling and home repairs in payment. Oh, and lawn maintenance and pest control."

"Sounds like you don't get much time off, Mike."

"Oh, can't complain. Lots of folks out there have it much worse. We have our health and beautiful children and food on the table. Know what I mean?"

"I know exactly what you mean," said Marly, shooting a furtive look toward Jack that told him she questioned very much whether *he* did.

Wonderful. The very things that drew most women to him—his money and power—caused the one he *wanted* to look at him sideways. Lyons continued to yak into his ear about issues that could easily have waited until tomorrow.

"So do you carry pictures of your children?" Marly asked Mike.

"Sure do." He dug into his back pocket for his wallet and passed them back to her.

"They're adorable."

Yeah, they were. But Jack didn't necessarily want her focused on them. "Lyons," he said into his cell phone, "I have to go. Brief me on this in the morning. I've got a date right now."

"Date?" squawked Lyons. "What do you not understand about what I'm telling you, Jack? The people see you as a playboy—"

Jack shut the phone and put it in his pocket.

Marly obviously liked Mike, since she'd offered to paint portraits of his kids sometime. She pulled a card out of her little tapestry bag and wrote her home number on the back for him.

Jack glared at Mike. Impossible, but he was jealous of his chauffeur! She hadn't hesitated a bit before giving *him* her contact information, while Jack *still* didn't have it.

He folded his arms across his chest.

"Something wrong, sir?" Mike met his eyes in the rearview mirror.

"No, no. Nothing's wrong." *Besides the fact that my date would rather be sitting up front with you.* His displeasure seemed to affect the atmosphere in the limo, though. Like black ink from a squid, it clouded the waters.

"Sir?" Mike said. "There's a bottle of champagne chilling in the ice bucket back there."

"Thanks. Marly, can I pour you a glass?"

She hesitated. "Sure."

The woman didn't want to sip champagne in a limo? What was wrong with her? How could he turn things around, elevate the mood a bit?

Jack produced two chilled glasses and filled them, handing one to Marly. She took it with thanks, but looked regretfully at Mike, as if she felt bad that Jack didn't ask him to join them in a toast.

"Mike's on duty," he reminded her. "And he's driving."

"Of course," she said quickly.

Jack hit the button that raised the divider, feeling like a jerk. But that was irrational! He and Marly were on a date. Yes, Mike's kids were cute, and yes, Mike was an all-around great guy, but Jack didn't want him in the picture right now.

"To dinner together," he said, raising his glass to her. "Cheers."

She kept her face utterly expressionless. "Cheers."

They drank, and Jack unaccountably thought of the time during his childhood when his mother had given him "grown-up ginger ale" to drink. He smiled.

"What?" Marly asked.

"I was just thinking of my mom." *Oh, brilliant thing to say, Jack, on a date.*

"Your mom?" She raised her eyebrows.

"The first time she gave me champagne. She called it ginger ale for grown-ups. I was twelve."

Marly smiled. "You...have a good relationship with your mother?"

"Oh, yeah. She's fabulous. My mom could run the country single-handed and still keep her sense of humor."

"That's high praise."

He shrugged. "It's the truth. What's yours like?"

She stared into her champagne glass for a moment too long. "Oh, you know. Ma's...retired now. She used to work for the post office."

"Yeah? What does she do in her spare time?"

Again, that infinitesimal hesitation. "Um, this and that. She has a bunko group and she watches her soaps."

Jack beat a conversational retreat, realizing that this topic was a sensitive one. "How about your dad?"

Marly brightened. "He's into everything he can do. Loves to fish, tends a garden, plays penny poker with the guys." She chuckled. "Gets passionate about politics— dyed-in-the-wool Democrat—and writes rude ditties that he plays on a guitar while he sits on his workbench."

"He sounds great," said Jack. "Well, except for the poor political judgment." He grinned. "Any brothers or sisters?"

Marly started to shake her head and then stopped. "Yeah, a rabid cat named Fuzzy who thinks he rules the house."

Jack pulled a long face. "Sounds like you and Fuzzy have a little sibling rivalry going."

"You could say that," Marly agreed, sipping more champagne.

"Would you like to lie down on ze couch and tell me all about it?" Jack asked in his best Dr. Freud voice.

She laughed. "Fuzzy has anger management issues and a lot of pent-up hostility. He's a psychopath, a Ninja and a master thief."

"Hmm," said Jack in a thoughtful tone. "He sounds like a prime candidate for, say, the CIA. Black ops?"

"If he gets shot at and thrown out of airplanes, then I'm all for drafting him. Can you write up an executive order right away?"

"Done," he said promptly. "Anything for you, beautiful." Jack picked up the champagne bottle and refilled her glass and his own.

"Thank you. Where are we headed? Canada?"

"We'll arrive at the surprise location shortly."

"You're not taking me to dine at the governor's mansion? I'm crushed."

"No, you're not. You'd hate the mansion. It's very stuffy. Not your style."

"How do you know that?" She looked surprised.

"I just do."

A wary expression crossed her face. "Been reading my file again, Hammer?"

He shook his head. "Nope. This is based purely on instinct. And if I'm right, you have to give me another kiss."

She frowned at him and drank more champagne. "Where are Frick and Frack?"

"Jimmy and Rocket are in a car—"

"Rocket? You've got to be kidding me."

"—behind us. Forget about them."

"They're too big to forget about. How do you live like this?"

Jack shrugged. "It is what it is."

"Do they follow you into the men's room, too? Watch you brush your teeth and put on your pajamas?"

"I don't wear pajamas," he told her. "I sleep in the nude." He laughed at her reaction to that. "And no, Jimmy and Rocket are *not* in the room."

"Did they really think that I might murder you with my texturing shears?"

"Marly, they're trained to protect me. They have to think about the possibilities—because I sure as hell don't want to."

She absorbed this in silence. "You live a very odd life, Jack."

He shrugged. "The life of political figures and celebrities everywhere."

"Well, I think it's sad." She stared out the window of the limo while Jack admired her profile, wanting to twist his fingers in the tiny curls she'd engineered to fall near one ear. The dangly silver earrings she wore called attention to her long, graceful neck. He wanted to trail kisses down it.

She reminded him of his great-great-grandmother's cameo, and awoke a sense of urgency in him. Urgency not to let her go, not to screw this up. An urgency to repeat history.

But so far the date was going less than swimmingly. He was jealous of his chauffeur, he'd talked about his mom, and Marly had expressed *pity* for his lifestyle. Yeah, he was SuperStud, all right. What else would go wrong tonight?

8

THE LIMOUSINE CARRIED them across the bridge to Key Biscayne and turned down a private drive that took them to the steps of a gargantuan Mediterranean mansion.

Marly had only seen houses like this one in the movies or on a paid tour, such as the time she'd gone to Newport, Rhode Island. She stared at the mansion, expecting Ingrid Bergman or Audrey Hepburn to come gliding down the steps in a tragically chic hat.

But Mike was opening the door and handing *her* out, and Jack took her arm to guide her inside. Even if the place had been decorated by Kmart, it would have been stunning architecturally. The very scale of it, the way the space was designed and the richness of the details took her breath away.

But it wasn't decorated at all—or at least, not beyond the foyer, which was populated by bad reproductions of Roman statues, all heroically endowed and naked as the day they were chiseled. Well, except…

One of the males wore a Marlin's baseball cap, another, a Groucho Marx nose and glasses. The females sported hats, too: one a floppy beach hat and the other a chic vintage cloche.

Marly burst out laughing and turned to Jack, who leaned against a pillar, just watching her. "Is this your house?"

"It will be, once I leave the governor's mansion. As you can tell, it needs a little work. The previous owners had…interesting taste."

"So," she said, gesturing at the statues with her thumb, "are they joining us for dinner?"

His lips twitched. "No. The table is only set for two." He took her elbow again and led her deeper into the house. In the center of the place was a huge open space, surrounded by a picture gallery. Two sets of stairs led down to the lower level of the house, which contained a library, a billiards room, a vast wet bar with room for every kind of liquor imaginable.

What am I doing here? Marly asked herself, feeling as if she were on the set of a movie. The whole house felt unreal to her. She thought of her parents' home, small and basic and comfortable; her mother's fondness for mass-manufactured knickknacks. Then she felt guilty for contrasting the two homes.

The most spectacular thing on the lower level of this mansion was the view: straight out behind an elegant, patterned, hardwood deck was the ocean. No guardrail marred the expanse of blue-green water, which occasionally lapped up through the planks and swept over them.

On the deck a white-draped table set for two sparkled in the evening sun with china, crystal and silver.

Marly gasped with pleasure as they walked outside. To the left, the deck ran down wide, shallow steps to a snaking river of a swimming pool, twice the length of an Olympic-size one and rimmed by gorgeous landscaping.

"I had the stone cherubs and swans surgically removed," said Jack. "They were overrunning the place and made all-too-convenient targets for birds."

"What, no well-endowed, shy nymphs?"

"I ditched the nymphs, too. They were definitely well-endowed, but not shy—in fact, they bordered on pornographic."

"Money definitely can't buy taste, huh?"

"So true."

"But, Jack, why didn't you have them all removed at once? Why are the ones in the front hall still there?"

He looked pained. "Because those are actually bolted to the floor, believe it or not. And we're waiting for the new marble to come in before removing them." He pulled out one of the chairs for her and she sat at the table. He sat opposite her.

Moments later a man in dark slacks and a guayabera shirt appeared with a chilled bottle of white wine in a silver ice bucket, along with two glasses. He poured for both of them and then went back inside.

"Jack, I can't believe I'm sitting here with you." Marly took a sip of her wine, drinking in the view, too. The ocean breeze blew over her skin like a caress, carrying reality away. She could almost hear her father, though, telling her not to be impressed. That most family fortunes had been built on the backs of the poor and repressed—people like them.

"Why not?" he asked. He smiled at her and she wanted to fall into his warm, open expression, wrap it around her like a blanket. She resisted, feeling guilty.

"Because we live such different lives. I wake up in an apartment each morning. You wake up in the governor's mansion. I cut people's hair. You cut people's taxes. I veto mullets. You veto legislation."

Jack laughed. "What I love about you is your fresh perspective on things." He settled lazily back in his chair, his hair lifting off his forehead in the wind. He looked carefree, privileged and faintly decadent. He also looked sexy as hell.

Marly raised her glass to her lips and tried not to notice that aspect of him, but it was more or less impossible. Jack's shirt was open at the neck, and she could see a few dark curly hairs beckoning her closer. She shut her eyes, trying not to remember just how spectacular that chest was, or how she'd been tempted more than once to sweep her fingers through those hairs and sample their texture and the heat of his skin beneath.

When she opened them, Jack was smiling at her. "This date," he said, "is finally going the way I want it to."

She supposed he was referring to the awkwardness in the limo, but she wasn't sure. "How, exactly, is that?"

He was saved from having to answer by the appearance of the silent man in the guayabera shirt, who brought them each a delicate plate of hors d'óeuvres.

Jack said, "Thank you, Tomas," while Marly gazed at the perfect aperitifs on her plate. They looked too pretty to eat. Really, how could she spoil the presentation by touching it?

"You must have slaved in the kitchen for days," she said in a dry voice. "You shouldn't have."

"Oh, it was nothing," Jack assured her, and it was the first time anyone had ever told her that and meant it. Wouldn't it be easy to entertain with panache if you had a chef and a full staff of household help? She'd throw parties all the time.

Again, it served to underline the differences between them, and Marly wondered what the hell she was doing here. She didn't belong in this world. She'd enjoy it for tonight, but after that she needed to go reclaim reality.

"Please eat," Jack urged her. She picked up a mushroom cap and bit into the divine. Stuffed with an exotic blend of cheeses and delicate spices, it melted on her tongue. Her expression must have conveyed her opinion, because he nodded as if she'd complimented the food out loud.

"Tomas is a magician," he said. "He makes my life worth living."

She had to agree, as she slowly sampled everything on her plate and sipped her wine.

"Now this—" Jack spread his hands wide "—is my idea of the perfect evening."

It was. She pushed away her guilt and discomfort. Just this one perfect evening, this fantasy... Marly nodded.

She'd given herself up to bliss when a thunderous noise destroyed everything. It came from the right, where three teenagers on Jet Skis erupted from the canal between Jack's house and the house next door.

The buildings were by no means on top of each other, and they were screened by rows of trees and hedges— not to mention stucco walls—but nothing could drown the noise. The kids churned up the water, doing figure eights and circles, racing each other and playing chicken.

Jack jumped up from the table and yelled something at them, but of course they couldn't hear. He stalked back to the table and yanked a cell phone from his pocket. Marly heard him yell the words "Rocket" and "call up the damn parents," but the mood of their dinner was ruined, to say the least.

The kids began to emit war whoops on top of it all, and ignored him when he tried waving his arms to get their attention.

"Don't they know who lives next door to them?" she asked.

Jack looked sheepish. "Unfortunately not," he admitted. "I bought the house through a trust and I didn't put the word out, since I was trying to guard my privacy. So for all they know, I'm just some cranky businessman out to ruin their good time, the little jerks."

"We could go inside," she suggested.

"There's no furniture in there." He looked genuinely upset that their romantic evening had been spoiled.

She got up and tugged at his hand. "Come on, Jack. Let's get out of here. This ritzy stuff isn't really me, anyway. Tell you what—let's get back in the limo, order a pizza and go eat it on the beach somewhere."

"Order a pizza?" He looked scandalized. "Do you know what Tomas will do to me?"

"He'll get over it, won't he? Tell him to invite his own friends over to eat and inhale Jet Ski fumes."

Jack laughed in spite of himself. He hesitated. "Fine. But we're taking the wine with us."

They startled Mike in the foyer. He'd obviously planned on a long, solitary evening of…scrapbooking? Marly and Jack exchanged glances at the neat rows of photographs arranged to maximum advantage on colorful decorative sheets of acid-free paper.

They'd caught him with a pair of pink edging scissors in his hand, adding the final touches to a page featuring his daughter and her Tinkerbell Halloween costume.

Mike scrambled to his feet. "Sorry, sir—I, uh, thought you'd be a while, so I, um…"

"What *is* all this stuff?" Jack looked perplexed. "Never mind. Just give me the car keys. We're going to order a pizza from the limo."

It was Mike's turn to look pole-axed. But he dug into his pocket and handed over the keys. "I'll be right there, sir."

"Take your time."

Marly and Jack left the house and he unlocked the limo door for her, aiming an evil eye in the direction of the still audible Jet Skis. "Little pissants."

"Don't growl, Jack." She slid into the backseat of the limo with a laugh and then froze at the expression on his face. She looked down and saw that her sarong had separated at the side, leaving her leg completely exposed from the upper thigh on down.

She extended a hand to fix it, but he caught it in his own. "Please," he said. "Don't do that."

He held up a finger. "Hold that thought. I'll be right back." And he opened the driver's side door, jammed the keys in the ignition and started the car. Then he got in beside her and hit the lock button.

Marly's breathing quickened. "Jack—"

"I won't do anything you don't want me to do," he promised. Then he extended a finger and touched it to the exposed skin just under the knot of her sarong.

"I don't want you to—" But she stopped midsentence because it was a lie. The finger he trailed down her thigh left something like a burn in its wake. He caressed her calf with his palm and then stroked the back of her knee.

"You ever made love in a limousine?" he asked her softly, his voice husky and pouring over her nerves like whiskey over ice. She melted under it.

"No," she whispered.

"Would you like to?"

Yes. "I'm…not sure."

Jack moved from sitting beside her to the opposite seat, so they sat knee to knee. He took a sip from the glass of wine he still held, and then set it down.

She felt odd, sitting there with one leg completely covered and the other completely exposed. She also didn't know what exactly he could see under her sarong from that angle. She pressed her knees together.

Jack bent forward, his blue eyes burning into hers. She met him halfway, their mouths searing each other and their tongues mating in a sensual, private dance. She stole his breath and he stole hers, until they broke apart, both gasping for air.

"Marly." He ran a hand over his face. "We should take this slow." He traced her lips with his finger while outside their little cocoon, they felt Mike get into the front seat and heard his door close.

"I'm sure he's wondering where the hell we want to go," Jack said. "Any preferences?"

She shook her head.

"You want to order that pizza?"

"Not at the moment." She smiled.

"I think we're on the same page." Jack pressed a button and spoke to Mike. "I think we just want to drive. Anywhere. For a while."

"Yes, sir."

"Sorry about your scrapbooking," Marly added.

Embarrassed laughter. "My wife makes me do it. She says she's no good."

Jack let go of the button and returned to his exploration of Marly's mouth. "I'm no good, either."

"Yeah, I think that's what I like about you," she said, nipping his finger. *What am I doing? I'm about to go down a path that may lead straight to hell...not to mention to the Republican party.* To her, the party of the rich and deceitful and the painful past.

But she didn't care. She sank back into the leather seat and let Jack Hammersmith, forty-fourth governor of Florida, run his hands up and down her bare leg, stopping only a quarter of an inch shy of decency. She let him slip off her sandal, massage her naked foot, and drizzle it with champagne. Then she let him suck it off her silver-painted toes, an indescribable sensation that she'd never experienced before.

He reached for her other leg, but she took his hand and laced his fingers with hers. Then, with her free one she unbuttoned his shirt down to the navel and explored the terrain of that warm, broad chest.

His breathing quickened and his eyelids dropped to half-mast. She ran her thumb over a taut nipple, lightly abraded it, and he caught his lip between his teeth. She let go of his hand and tugged his shirt free of his waistband. He looked beyond sexy as he sat there, knees apart and shirt wide open. Republican, Democrat or alien life form, she wanted him more than she'd ever wanted any man.

He apparently felt the same way toward her, since he shrugged out of his shirt entirely and then hauled her onto his lap. He whipped off her silk tank, exposing a sheer, lacy black bra embroidered with silver thread. Jack groaned at the sight and cupped her breasts in his hands. "You are so beautiful." Then he touched his tongue, through the lingerie, to one pink nipple.

At the sensation, Marly whimpered and let her head fall back, pushing herself farther into Jack's hot mouth. It seemed to excite him, since he yanked the bra straps off her shoulders and down her arms, pushing the whole thing to her waist.

He turned her so that she straddled him and then devoured her breasts, tonguing and sucking her nipples, abrading them with his teeth and thumbs until she felt entirely liquid, her only points of consciousness under his mouth and the ache of longing between her thighs. She was beyond wet for him, half crazed with desire.

Jack's erection pushed at her, rubbed her through his pants, but when she reached for it he lifted her and set her back on her own seat across from him. She made a sound of protest, but he ignored her and dropped to his knees in front of her, spreading her own knees apart and pushing her sarong to one side.

He kissed and licked his way up her inner thighs while she almost orgasmed just due to anticipation of what he was about to do. The engine of the limo roared under them as the car picked up speed.

"Are you wet for me?" asked Jack.

"Yes," she managed to say.

"Are you hot?"

She nodded.

"Almost over the edge?"

She could feel his breath at the core of her and could no longer speak. She dug her hands into his shoulders, instead. Then, inexplicably, he pulled away. The next thing she felt was the icy champagne bottle between her legs, right where his hot breath had been a moment before.

He pressed it against her panties and Marly froze on the edge of climax.

9

JACK GAVE HIS BEST diabolical laugh as she shrieked and twisted to get away. He removed the bottle, set it back in the ice bucket and captured Marly's wrists before she could plant a fist in his eye.

Then he put his face back between her thighs and touched his tongue to her through her silver-embroidered, black lace panties. They were damp with her need, and that excited him almost as much as the way she was twisting to avoid him at the moment. She was annoyed, outraged and didn't want to succumb again.

But as he slid his tongue along the rough lace he could also feel soft, warm, feminine flesh, and it quivered under the sensual assault.

The scent of her drove him wild, made him want to rip off everything she wore and throw her down on the seat, plunging in and out of her until he was half dead. But first he wanted, in a very primitive way, to master her and to make her need him.

She was already making soft, feminine noises of helpless pleasure and no longer trying to avoid his mouth. So he released her wrists and pulled her panties aside with a finger, sliding under them, licking and teasing and sucking.

She began to raise her hips toward him and rock in an unconscious rhythm of desire. Jack considered the awkward alternative for half a second, rejected it and then ripped her panties in half in one easy motion.

He now had unfettered access to her and he gave her all he had, plunging his tongue into her with abandon and exquisite torture until she came apart, thrashing against his mouth. Jack loved the sight.

He wanted to take her right then, ride the aftershocks of her orgasm, but he restrained himself and watched her return slowly to consciousness. Her eyes flew open, met his and then closed with an expression of utter mortification. Jack wiped his mouth and chin on his shirt and then kissed her, both to dissipate her embarrassment and to show her that far from disgusting him, she'd turned him on.

Still without speaking, he guided her hand to his cock, which was so hard it was painful. She unzipped his pants and took him into her hands while he tried not to slobber with pleasure. Tried not to just grab her and jam himself inside her without any grace or regard for what she wanted.

But Marly sat in his lap and rubbed herself on him, back and forth until he thought he'd die. "Condom?" she whispered.

He pulled his wallet from his pants and dug out a packet. She took it from him and rolled it on.

Then she rose over him and sank down in one fluid motion, tilting his world on its axis.

Erotic lightning streaked through him as she engulfed his cock, a hot, wet, feminine fist—and then began to move on him, up and down, stroking and caressing every inch.

Jack would have liked to remain in control. But she ripped it from him and he could do nothing but drive himself into her with relentless need, gripping her bottom and trying to brace her.

She started to make wild, keening cries that tore at his bid for loss of consciousness. "I'm hurting you," he said against her hair.

"No," she gasped. "Stop and I will rip your head off."

Even through a fog of cresting lust, Jack understood that to be encouragement, and when she locked her ankles around the small of his back and actually kicked her heels into his kidneys, he pumped into her fast and furious until he exploded inside her.

"Jack, Jack, don't stop," she begged. And though his eyes were crossed and he was pretty sure his climax had blown his cock right off, he obliged with what had to be the mangled stump—until she arched her back, ground wildly against him and then went limp in his arms.

He slowly registered that they were half naked in the back of the limo and looked quite ridiculous. Marly's bra was still around her waist and he had his shoes, socks and pants on.

She opened her eyes and smiled at him. Her hair

billowed around her shoulders, her face was flushed and her lips swollen. She personified the best kind of sin.

Jack dropped a kiss on her nose as she climbed carefully off him. He did away with the condom and wrapped it in a napkin before disposing of it.

Marly started to pull her bra up and back into place, but he shook his head at her. "Give me that," he said, and used the special one-handed, strap-zapper technique he'd perfected in college. If a guy didn't know how to get a bra undone one-handed, he just had no finesse.

"What are you doing?" she asked, laughing.

He untied his shoes, ditched them and his socks. He unbuckled his belt and slipped out of his pants and boxers.

"I think we should finish the champagne while riding around butt-naked in the limo. You ever ridden around butt-naked in a limo?"

"No. I've never even been in a limo except for the one that took us to my grandmother's graveside from the funeral home."

Jack pursed his mouth. "Well, there's a cheery memory. Let's improve your outlook on limos, shall we?"

"I think we already have. I'd never had a screaming orgasm in a limo until today, either."

"First time for everything," said Jack, pouring two fresh glasses of champagne.

"Yeah," she said, giving him and the champagne bottle a filthy look.

"What?" he asked, blue eyes full of innocence.

"That was a dirty, dirty trick."

"But I made up for it, didn't I?"

"I'm thinking that only a Republican would pull something like that on a woman."

Jack started laughing. "Why do you say that?"

"Get 'em all hot and bothered, then apply the deep freeze in the name of morality."

"Hey," he said. "I didn't do anything in the name of morality. I did it in the name of hot, sweaty sex."

She crossed one long, lithe leg over the other and sat like a czarina in spite of the fact that she was naked. Her posture was that of a dancer, her body a work of sculpture. Jack wanted to run his hands over every inch of her smooth skin—not necessarily in a sexual way, but just for sensuality's sake.

He stared at the red rose she'd painted on that one toenail, fascinated at the detail she'd managed to incorporate. She'd used a darker color of red to add dimension and depth to it, and had even painted a dark green stem.

Like a Georgia O'Keeffe flower, the rose resonated with sex, hinted of dark velvet depths and extended an unspoken invitation to a man: explore at your leisure…but also at your own risk.

Jack got hard all over again. How could this woman turn him on with just a toenail? The idea was preposterous.

But she did.

And since he wasn't sitting like her, with his legs

crossed, his interest became immediately noticeable, winking at her with its one eye.

"Hello," said Marly, her lips twitching.

"What can I say?" Jack spread his hands, palms up. "He likes you. He's ready to go exploring again."

"In case he missed something the last time?"

"Yeah. Thoroughness is important to him."

"Gosh, how many condoms do you carry in your wallet at once?" Marly lifted an eyebrow.

"*Shit.* I hadn't thought about that." Crushed, Jack stared at her longingly.

She pulled her little bag over and unzipped the top of it. "Colored? Ribbed? Lubricated?"

He blinked at her. "Uh. How—how many do you have?"

She shrugged. "I'm not sure. I dumped some in my little makeup bag a while back. Why?"

"You're not *sure?*"

"That's what I said. What's the funny look for?"

"Meaning you don't remember how many encounters you've had?" Jack heard the suspicion and tinge of outrage in his voice, but somehow he couldn't control it.

"No." She glared at him. "Meaning I don't rememeber how many I put in there to begin with! Besides, my *encounters* are *so* none of your business."

"You just made them my business," he growled.

She actually pushed him with her foot. "Oh, did I? Well, but gosh, Governor, I thought all of that information would be in my file—down to the fact that I didn't even vote in the last election. Did you not do your homework? Because if you had, you'd know that I haven't been with anyone in over a year and a half." Clearly furious, Marly reached for her clothes.

"I'm sorry," Jack said. "I just—"

"Have a double standard? That it's okay for you to walk around with condoms, because you're a guy. But if I do, then I'm a slut?"

"No."

"That is so unbelievably…" She searched for words. *"Republican!"*

"It has nothing to do with my politics, Marly. It has to do with the simple fact that it made me jealous to think about you with other men. All right?"

"That's just—primitive."

"I'm a guy. We *are* primitive in certain ways."

"Jack, let me make something clear to you. Just because we've had sex does not mean that you possess me or something." She shook her head at him. *"That's* really Republican, too."

Jack ground his teeth. "No, it's human. And your sniping about my party is starting to get on my nerves. Wanna tell me where all that's coming from? Besides the fact that it's not 'cool' these days to be a Republican? I'm giving you credit for not being that shallow."

She shrugged and looked out the window. "You got elected on a conservative ticket, on promises to return family values to the state of Florida."

"Yeah?"

"You think your voters would approve of what we just did?"

"It's really not their business," said Jack. "But I'm unmarried, so are you. We practiced safe sex. We didn't expose ourselves to impressionable children—or even to adults for that matter. Again, where's this coming from?"

"You got elected, Jack, on a platform of reform that included sweeping statements about a return to morality."

"Yes," he agreed. "Why does that bother you?"

"Let's just say that there are a lot of people in your party, a lot of people who have supported you, who are…intolerant."

"That doesn't necessarily mean that I share their views. Getting the nomination to run for office is all about compromise. It means that I can't necessarily push my personal agenda, I have to push for the party's agenda."

"Doesn't that bother you?"

"Hell yes, sometimes it bothers me. But it's the reality of politics." He put a hand on her arm. "Marly, there are days when I absolutely hate what I do. Of course, if you ever quote me on that I'll categorically deny it."

"I wouldn't quote you. But if you hate it so much, then why do you do it?"

"It's complicated. It's about stepping up to the plate and taking responsibility. If I don't do it, there are plenty of other people willing to take my place—but not always for the right reasons. I have been blessed with a certain amount of charisma, heart, integrity and leadership ability. I can get things done, and most of the time I can get them done without pissing off too many people unnecessarily. And I care about Florida. I guess that's what it all boils down to—I may hate my job sometimes, but I care too much to walk away."

Marly had to respect that, but she sighed. "My dad once went against family tradition and crossed over to your side, you know. Until he and our whole town were betrayed by one of your party's finest. Patrick Compton, upstanding state representative. Spewed all kinds of promises, anything anyone wanted to hear.

"We elected him to see after our interests up there in Tallahassee, and he sold us out. He was in bed with a huge fruit corporation, whose name I will not mention. And that huge corporation made it impossible for our farmers to compete with them price-wise. They were all going bankrupt.

"The Pattywhacker came to town and promised them all job stability if they'd sell out to this fruit company. Most of them didn't have a lot of choice but to trust him and do it. So they sold, on the understanding that they'd keep their jobs.

"Within six months, the company used a loophole they called 'moral perishability' and shut down every operation. Closed them and stripped them of assets. Took off, leaving the town to die—because its residents had all worked in the citrus industry.

"My dad—" Marly's voice cracked. "My dad, who

had the pride of twenty men, *died inside* the day he had to go on welfare, but his military pension wasn't enough to keep us going."

"Marly," Jack said quietly, "I'm sorry. I'm sorry that happened to your family—"

"Guess who got a fat consulting contract with the big fruit company six months later?"

"—but is it fair to blame the entire party for the actions of one individual?"

"That's not the only story like that out there, Jack, and you know it."

"There are Democrat creeps, too, Marly. You're generalizing and stereotyping."

"Don't tell me that! What happened to us and to our town was very specific. But if you're going to accuse me of generalizing, sure, let's go there! Republicans endorse big business, and big business encourages behavior like that. Everything's about the bottom line, screw the little people."

"It's called competition. Businesses have to pay attention to their bottom lines. They'll go belly-up if they don't. A business isn't a charity. Capitalism isn't socialism—though your tax-and-spend Democrats would sure like to change that, wouldn't they?"

Marly shook her sarong and top. "Yeah, God forbid any of us should have a heart and try to feed starving people or try to correct the injustices of society…." She wrapped the sarong around her lower body and shrugged into the top.

Jack sighed. "Society will never be perfect, Marly.

It's composed of human beings, not angels. The government cannot fix everything—nor should it be expected to."

"Interesting philosophy, coming from the mouth of someone who ran on a platform of restoring morality to the state!" She grabbed her ripped panties and bra and shoved them into her tiny tapestry bag. "Please take me home."

"Marly—"

"Please."

His jaw tight, a pulse jumping in the side of his neck, Jack hit the button that allowed him to communicate with Mike. He gave the instruction and then got dressed himself in silence.

They went for long minutes without speaking. Finally he said, "So the gist of this little talk is that you're calling me a hypocrite."

"I didn't say—"

"Yes, you pretty well did say it. So now you can listen to me. I've given up years of my life to public service. I do the best I can. I'm there in the trenches actively doing something. And you know what pisses me off more than anything, Marly? It's people like you, who rant and rave about politics but don't lift a finger to try to do anything.

"You like to sit around and blame the Republicans for being the root of all evil? That's just great. You don't like what we stand for, then get out and work for the other side. But don't you dare treat me with disrespect if you're not even voting on state issues. And how about all those social injustices you want rectified, sweetheart. Why don't you get off that pretty little ass of yours and go raise some funds?"

With flawless timing, Mike brought the limo to a stop just outside her apartment complex. Marly looked daggers at Jack, glared at him as if she'd be glad to dig out his still-beating heart with a pair of shears.

Jack didn't flinch. He stared right back at her. He might still desire her for reasons beyond him, but he wasn't going to take her canned left-wing crap.

For a moment he thought she might actually slap him.

Instead she took a deep breath and slipped on her shoes. "I'd like to say something incredibly rude to you right now," she said in a low voice. Then she paused. "But I can't, because—damn you—you're right."

And without waiting for Mike, Marly opened the door of the limo and slipped out.

10

MARLY SLAMMED her apartment door and threw her tapestry bag onto the couch. She stood in her living room, staring into the filmy curtains that covered her sliding-glass doors, able to see the roofs of the factory buildings in spite of them.

Jack Hammersmith was too damned good looking and way too amazing in bed (or limo seat). She didn't particularly care for the way he'd challenged her. She was used to the comfort of being agreed with by her fellow liberal friends, not criticized for her political apathy.

She really didn't want to think about how lazy she'd been during the last elections; how because it had been pouring rain she'd put off going to the polls until she barely had time to make it...and then taken a client at the last minute so that she *hadn't* made it.

Her dad would have been ashamed of her. Quite frankly, she was ashamed of herself. After all, she'd been lucky enough to be born in a democracy where people were free to choose their leaders. She didn't have to get involved in the particulars of how that democracy operated on the local and state levels, but she *did* have an obligation to vote.

Otherwise, she was really ceding her right to have opinions. She was saying, through her inaction, that it was okay for decisions to be made without her input. She was accepting the rule of someone else without question. Ugh.

Marly had never had any problem looking in the mirror before. She'd always been proud of her decision to help her father, and proud of the fact that she was good at her job and lived a stable lifestyle—since a lot of people she knew didn't.

But now as she turned to walk into her bedroom and caught sight of herself in the big oval mirror over her dresser, she grimaced.

Jack, the jerk, was right. He was right about a lot of things—that she was guilty of stereotyping, that she hadn't really bothered to find out what he was all about before labeling him "Republican: yuck." And he was right that someone who didn't get involved had no business criticizing those who did.

If she really got down to brass tacks, she'd probably have to admit that she wasn't terribly well informed about most of the issues he dealt with every single day.

After all, half listening to a network morning news program while she aimed a blow-dryer at her head didn't exactly qualify as in-depth research. She resolved to do better and to read a newspaper regularly.

She closed her eyes and could still feel Jack's lips on hers, hear his voice in her ears. She could feel where he'd been elsewhere, too, on—and in—her body.

She opened her eyes and stared into the mirror. She looked normal and average, not like the kind of woman who had wild monkey sex with the governor in a limo.

Marly walked into the bathroom, started the water running in her tub and lit a candle. She poured some bubble bath into the water, shrugged out of her clothes and slipped into warm, scented bliss. This would be the only time she'd have to herself for the next week, because of the salon's extended hours and her growing client list.

Being written up in *Shore* magazine had been fantastic for business, but she was starting to feel a little frazzled. Once word got out that she was styling Jack Hammersmith's hair, she'd be getting even more calls.

Marly told herself not to complain—being in demand was fantastic. A compliment. A vote of confidence. And it brought in more money to pay off her father's medical bills.

If only being in demand weren't quite so tiring.

IN ORDER TO accommodate the flood of new clients over the next two weeks, Marly began multitasking. She began to cut one client's hair while another was waiting for color to set under the dryer. She finished the color client while an assistant dried and styled the first client's hair. She skipped lunch in favor of Red Bull and protein bars.

She started having to skip dinner, too. A painting she'd begun a month ago sat in a corner of her apartment, just a sketch with a few smears of color. And to top it all off, she hadn't heard from Jack. He was done with her, then. So much for her being The One.

She didn't want to think about the fact that she had been extremely rude about his politics. Maybe he just needed time to cool off.

New vitamin packs mixed into her morning orange juice helped for a while, but she still felt ragged, almost destroyed, by the end of each "day." Her days ended at midnight and began again at 8:00 a.m. Her career was becoming a brilliant success, but her life had evolved to merely an existence.

It was on one of her manic, multitasking days at the salon that she heard again from Jack.

Shirlie scrambled across the room, her baby-blue miniskirt rucked up, only one earring on, and the cordless phone glued to the bare ear. "Marly!"

"Yes?" Her mouth was full of metal clips and she was working on a new customer's highlights.

"Governor Hammersmith is coming on the line! Here."

Her first instinct was anger that he'd waited so long to call. Her second was that she didn't have time to talk to him. "Shirl," Marly said around the clips, "I can't take it right—"

Shirlie made a noise of exasperation and jammed the phone at the side of her head.

"Uh," Marly said. "Hello?"

"Is this my favorite bleeding heart liberal?" Jack's voice boomed.

"Yeah, but she can't really talk right now."

"Not even to one of the leaders of the free world?"

Her client jabbed her in the stomach with an index finger. "Are you crazy?" she asked. "The governor? Go talk to him. I can wait."

Thank you, Marly mouthed at her. Then she walked with the phone to the kitchenette, while Shirlie went running to the front to answer another line. What did Jack want? Whatever it was, she didn't have any more minutes in the day to accommodate him.

"What's up, Jack?" Though she didn't want to admit it, her heart was galloping around in her chest. "Have you passed a new law that declares open season on Jet Skis?"

He laughed. "I'm working on it. Listen, I need you to fly to Tallahassee to cut my hair."

"What?" *Oh, right. I'm going to give you a whole day to do that! You've got a nerve, buddy.*

"I have a TV interview in a couple of days. So do you think you could make it up here either this evening or tomorrow? I'll send the Gulfstream for you."

You'll send the Gulfstream. Of course—like it's a yellow cab. "Jack, I have thirteen different appointments between now and midnight tomorrow night."

"I don't suppose there's any way to reschedule those? Because there's a *great* little French restaurant I was going to take you to, and I have tickets to a play."

It did sound wonderful. Marly hesitated. "I'd love to, but I can't reschedule that many people unless it's a total emergency. It's too much revenue lost for the salon—and for me."

Jack was silent for a moment. "Well, if it's a question of money, I can make it up to you."

It's not just a question of money, Marly thought. *It's a question of presumption! You and your play tickets are not more important than thirteen other people, even though you're the governor and you're hot and I'd love to see you again—in spite of the fact that you're a Republican.*

"Jack, I can't let you do that and you know it. But thank you for the offer."

"Why not?" he asked.

"Jack. You can't seriously expect me to drop everything just for a whim of yours! Especially after you've left me hanging for two weeks."

Again, a pause ensued, as if he were just realizing he'd been inconsiderate. "I'm sorry. I didn't mean to leave you hanging. I've been busy and I lost track of time. Well, if you can't come here, I'll just have to come in to After Hours, then. Can you clear a spot for me?"

"Give me a second to look at the book, okay?"

"Yup," he said.

She ran to the reception desk and grabbed the book from Shirlie, scanning furiously for any open time.

She said, "Come at four tomorrow. I think I can reschedule someone. Okay?"

"I don't suppose you can squeeze in dinner afterward?"

"No. I'm sorry. Give me a little more notice next time."

"All right. Your schedule's as packed as mine." Jack paused. "Hey…about our last date. I'm sorry if I was a little blunt."

Two apologies. She was impressed. "It's okay. I deserved it. I'd been making snarky comments about the Dark Side all night."

She heard choked laughter on his end of the line. "Excuse me? Did you just say *the Dark Side?*"

"Yes. But I can't get into an argument with you right now, no matter how tempting it is, because I have to go before my client's hair turns purple. See you tomorrow, Jack." And she pressed the off button.

Wow. I just hung up on the governor. Does that make me bad-ass or what? Marly walked calmly back to her client.

"Thank you for your patience," she said.

"Ohmigod!" the woman squealed. "So are you cutting Jack Hammersmith's hair?"

Marly nodded.

"I can't wait to tell my friends that I share the governor's hairdresser! I am so excited!"

Marly smiled.

"So is he a good tipper?"

She nodded. "He left me a tip the size of Alaska the first time I cut his hair."

"Well, sorry, hon." The woman winked at her. "I can only afford Rhode Island."

THE APPEARANCE of Jack Hammersmith at After Hours the next day caused quite a stir, not least because the Fabulous Four was there and already on their third glass of wine—which the salon had *not* offered them. Denise, the only brunette of the bunch, had a habit of getting up and fetching the bottle "because I don't want to bother you gals."

Marly, Nicky and the shampoo girls knew very well that this was a transparent ploy to help themselves to more free wine, but they didn't say anything as long as the designated driver for the day didn't look too plowed.

After Hours was a fun, preparty hot spot, but it wouldn't be for long if they got sued for causing someone's drunk driving accident. So far they'd only had to steal the Fab Four's keys once. Pretending total ignorance of where they could be, Alejandro had called the ladies a cab and avoided both an ugly scene and responsibility for turning them loose on Miami's freeways.

Today, three of the Fab Four were lined up at the manicure stations while one of them was having her eyebrows and lip waxed.

It was Rebecca who screeched as she saw the governor. "Ohmigod! It's Jack Hammersmith!"

"Ohmigod! Ohmigod!" the others chorused.

Denise, behind the curtain that separated the waxing area, screamed, "Where?" She popped her head around the drape.

"There—*ooooh*, honey. Not a good look for you," Rebecca whispered, shaking her head.

"What? Oh." Denise had a large waxing strip on the right side of her upper lip. She looked a bit bizarre, but she checked out Jack thoroughly before disappearing again.

Rebecca was even bolder. She snatched up her manicurist's ticket pad and had taken three steps toward
Jack when Jimmy and Rocket cut her off and blocked
her. "Step away from the governor, ma'am."

"But I only wanted—I was just trying to get his autograph."

"Easy there, Rebecca," Marly said. "Frick and Frack
tend to get antsy when people rush the governor. Especially when they're armed with a ticket pad and a
pen. Didn't you ever see *Grosse Point Blank*? You can
kill someone with a pen."

Jack snorted with laughter as Jimmy and Rocket
gave her a death stare. He cruised right over, dipped her
as if he were Fred Astaire, and kissed her senseless in
front of God and everyone. "I've missed you," he said
into her ear.

"You can't *do* that!" said Marly, struggling upright
and pushing him away.

"What? This?" And Jack planted another one on
her. "Why not?"

The entire salon was staring at them, and by now
Frick and Frack were probably running remote ballis-
tics tests on the tube of lipstick in her pocket. "Jack!"

"I can't help it," he told her. "You're just so beautiful."

It was such an easy line for him to deliver, and
maybe she was getting sappy over him, but her heart
turned over. Still, it was embarrassing to be kissed
in front of all her clients and coworkers, and the
gossip was going to spread within hours, if not
minutes.

"You know," she told him, "it's probably not going to do your reelection campaign any good if you're seen kissing random hairstylists all over Miami."

Jack stared down at her, his eyes very blue. "I'm not kissing random hairstylists. I'm kissing *you*. And I'm not that worried about it. There are no reporters here that I can see."

"Go sit in the chair in the back room, or you're going to get swarmed for your autograph. I can see that I'm already going to have to get it for Rebecca, which means at least three others."

Jack shrugged good-naturedly and walked over to Rebecca. "Hi, I'm Jack Hammersmith."

"I know!" she breathed, half swooning. Her tongue was falling *out* of her bright red mouth and her hair was falling *into* it. "Can I—? Would you?" She handed him the tablet and pen. "For Rebecca."

He scrawled his name for her, and predictably, the rest of the Fab Four waited in line, too, along with Nicky and the shampoo girls.

Marly pinched Nicky's arm as she walked by him. "Behave!" she snapped.

Moi? he mouthed. *Of course!*

Today he wore ironed blue jeans with purple lips embroidered on the left rear pocket and a T-shirt that said Tender across the chest.

After Denise, Rebecca and the rest of the Fab Four had finished telling Jack about how much they admired him, Nicky cut to the chase. "God, what a shame that you're straight."

Jack blinked and produced a smile. He shook Nicky's hand and scrawled his signature.

The stylist opened his mouth to say something else, but Marly grabbed his arm and dragged him away. "You said you were going to behave!"

"I am. I didn't ask him out, did I?" Nicky put his hand on his hip. "I'm on my very best behavior, doll."

"Oy." She got her equipment and followed Jack into the back.

He said in plaintive tones, "I'd much rather get naked with you than get a haircut."

"Forget it," she told him. "After your little performance out there, everybody in this whole place is going to notice if I have a single makeup smudge when I come out of here. And they'll be checking your collar for lipstick, too."

She took a critical look at his hair. "What exactly do you want me to do?"

"Oh, well, you know. It's just a little long." He smiled at her with too much innocence.

"You know, if you weren't a man of many responsibilities, like, oh, say, the governance of this state, I might suspect that you made up this hair emergency as an excuse to see me."

He cocked his head. "*Noooooo*. Surely you don't think that."

She folded her arms across her chest and nodded. "I do."

"Well, I did try to get you to come to me. But you've got that workaholic thing going. It's *so* annoying."

She was tempted to smack him, but he was just too good-looking. He had a young Mel Gibson's power over women.

"So you see, if the affairs of the state grind to a screeching halt today, it's all your fault."

"I don't think so!"

"Well, here's the hair emergency. I think my dark roots are showing under the gray."

"No, they're not."

"If you come closer and check, you'll see what I mean."

Marly walked over to him, leaned forward and inspected his head—while he took advantage of the situation by sliding his hands up under her skirt.

"Jack!"

"Yes?" His big warm hands were cupping her cheeks now, feeling amazing and turning her on—even though she was borderline angry with him.

"You had me reschedule a client for this?"

"Yeah," he said, sliding his fingers under the elastic of her panties and inward, taunting her and teasing with feather-like touches.

She wanted, again, to smack him—but couldn't. Because her breath was coming too fast and too shallow to gather the necessary oxygen.

Jack used the unfair advantage to tug her onto his lap, spread her knees and get more detailed about his exploration.

"Jack, you cannot just show up here and—and—" Her head fell back.

"And?" he prompted, shoving her shirt up and getting personal on other levels, too.

"—doooo this!" She managed to get the words out, her eyes now closed.

"Would you like me to stop?"

She shook her head. Sensations streaked through her and she pushed against his fingers, his palm, his wicked heat.

"Because I will if you want me to. We Republicans are gentlemen, you know, in spite of all our other failings—like being level-headed and fiscally responsible and against the growth of monolithic government bureaucracy, bound in miles of red tape…"

"Jack?"

"Hmm?"

"Shut up and unzip your pants!"

"I thought you'd never ask." And the governor proceeded to show her what a perfect gentleman he really was, condom and all. He picked her up and set her on the white marble sink, which felt deliciously cold against her bare bottom. Then he rolled on a condom and slid inside her, kissing her lips at the same time.

"I couldn't stay away, Marly. You do something to me. Even when you're rude. You looked so hot stomping away from the car…so mad at the fact that you had to admit I was right."

"You're the only person I'm rude to," she said, gasping for air. She angled her hips and pushed against him. "It's not really something I'm proud of."

"You got a little disrespect-for-authority thing going

there, sweetheart?" He cupped her breasts and played havoc with her nipples.

"Ahhhhh." She let her head fall back again and arched her back. "I guess so."

He slid his hands under her backside and drove into her hard, making her squeak. When she could breathe again, she said, "You got a thing going for bohemian, braless girls in gypsy skirts?"

"Absolutely."

"But I'm so not your type."

"How do you know what my type is?"

"Come on—I read the papers and the occasional gossip rag."

"Don't—" Jack drove in "—believe—" he pulled out "—everything—" he slid in again "—you read—" and came out "—in the papers." He impaled her on the last words, staring her down with those blue eyes.

Marly felt the faucet digging into her back as the first eddies of her orgasm started deep within her pelvis. Jack maneuvered out again, managing to stroke her with his cock in erotic places she didn't know she had.

The tremor inside her seemed to follow his action, streaked after him and then got shoved back up against her inner walls when he drove in again. He moved his hips in a circle, and spread her thighs even wider. She was coming, ready or not.

As he repeated the circular motion, she disintegrated completely, mind and body swept away by a rainbow of color and bliss. He sealed her cries with his lips and knocked the faucet out of the way, protecting her spine.

Then he, too, pumped into her wildly and lost control. His stiffening, the stilling of his hips and a long, quiet groan in her ear told Marly that he'd made it.

They remained that way for a few moments, unable to move. Marly raised her head and noticed that he still wore his shirt and tie, dress slacks, socks, shoes—everything. She'd just had sex with a Suit. He looked immaculate, except for the unzipped pants and the condom, still buried inside her along with his cock.

Marly began to laugh. "Is this how Republicans have sex? In pin-striped suits?"

Jack nodded. "Yeah." He twitched inside her, and she used her internal muscles to squeeze him.

"Hey! Give it back," he ordered.

"Nope. It's trespassing in Democratic territory now. I've arrested it and it's in jail."

Jack's hands tightened on her ass. "Cushiest jail I've ever been in, honey. Mmm. Tell me what laws to break so you'll arrest me again, okay?" He pulled out and lifted her off the sink, setting her on her feet.

She wobbled on rubbery legs for a moment, pulling her skirt down and staring at his tie. "Next time, you ditch the suit and tie before we, um—"

"Before we make love?"

"—have sex."

He nodded and grinned. "Okay, done. I'm fine with that—because you just agreed that there's gonna be a next time, without me even asking." And Jack Hammersmith, playboy governor, gave her a sexy-as-hell wink as he zipped up his pants.

11

MARLY HOPED THAT Frick and Frack were deaf as posts, but she had a bad feeling that their hearing was just fine. How she had managed to forget their existence and boink the governor while they stood just outside the treatment room, she didn't know.

They wore little ear thingies that undoubtedly connected them to some kind of radio, and she just prayed that they were listening to loud, obnoxious Security Detail Rap or something.

She'd forced Jack to sit in the chair and she'd wet his hair, then made some minor snips and shaved his neck. After all, they had to at least make it *look* as though she'd done his hair and not him.

Then she'd walked him to the front door of the salon after carefully checking to see that her skirt wasn't caught in her panties or anything. She even shook his hand and asked him if he'd like to make another appointment while his eyes danced privately for her.

"Well, I'd love to, Marly. You do such a good job."

"Thank you, Governor. We do try to make our clientele happy." She felt her color rising as his mouth twitched.

"Keeps us coming back for more."

She cleared her throat and avoided his gaze.

"So," he said, "why don't I call you—with my schedule, it can be hard to keep a regular time. Er—is there another number where I can reach you?"

He was asking for her home number again. Ridiculous, maybe, but she just didn't want to give it to him. She told herself that it was because she didn't feel like having Jimmy and Rocket listening in on her private line. But it probably had more to do with not wanting to stare at her home phone, waiting for the man to call. After all, he was Florida's number-one ladies' man. He'd probably be up for one more bout of sex and then he'd be off, sniffing after another skirt.

She needed to look at this situation in perspective; view it as exactly what it was, no more, no less. The governor was scratching his bohemian itch, no matter what he said about his great-great-grandfather and her being The One.

It's better to be an itch than a bitch, right?

Marly said, "Oh, you can just call me here at the salon. I'm always around." She handed him a business card, ignoring Shirlie's pointed stare and slap to her forehead.

The corners of Jack's mouth turned down for a moment, before he righted them for the public's benefit. Because the public, in the form of every single person in After Hours, was eating this up.

God, at least they don't know what we just did back there. Marly thanked the stars. She wore no makeup that he could have smudged, and she had done the skirt check and her top wasn't on inside out.

"Right," Jack said. "So I'll have my people get in touch and we'll arrange to fly you to Tallahassee next time. Say, in about a week?"

Behind her, Shirlie gave an excited squeak.

"Great. That—that will be just fine. Thank you, Governor."

"Call me Jack," he said, and flashed her one of those irresistible, panty-melting grins. But behind it his eyes were serious, and they reflected something she couldn't quite read...was it hurt?

"Thank you, Jack." She raised her hand and waggled her fingers at him.

"Thank *you,* darlin'." Jimmy opened the door for him, and Jack stepped through, followed by Rocket, who ripped his eyes with difficulty from Shirlie's twin attractions.

"Frick, Frack, it was sheer pleasure to see you again."

Curiously, they ignored her. Go figure. Marly turned, only to find that the eyes of everyone in the salon slid away from hers. What was up with that?

Nicky swooped down on her and dragged her into the back. "Cutie pie, come with Uncle Nicky."

"What? Why?"

He poked his tongue into his cheek and failed miserably at not grinning. "Because you need some emergency repairs, doll."

"I do?"

He winced and nodded. "I don't know what you and the Jackrabbit were doing back there, but the back of your head looks like someone scrubbed it with a Brillo pad."

Horrified, she put a hand to her braid, only to find that her hair wasn't so braided. It was pure, crazy fuzz starting about three inches above her nape.

"And I don't even want to ask what that red mark on your back is, but if I had to make a guess…"

If she'd ripped off her face and thrown it into a pan of sizzling oil, it couldn't be hotter. "Don't guess. Okay? Just don't." She moaned. "Everyone out there saw my hair, didn't they?"

Nicky glanced up at the ceiling. Then he glanced at the painted floor. Finally he slid his eyes toward hers. "Um, yeah."

"Don't you dare say a word. Just please, please, fix it."

"The Fab Four are schnockered. They probably won't remember," he offered. "And my client didn't have her glasses on, so she may not have noticed. But Shirlie definitely wants to know all about the gubernatorial goods, so to speak."

"Just shoot me, Nicky. Just put me out of my misery, okay?"

JACK KISSED HIS MOTHER on the cheek and admired her new sapphire earrings, an anniversary gift from his father the senator. "Mom, you look gorgeous. Where's Senior?"

"He's already on the verandah, puffing on a Cohiba. Darling, if I ever decide to take up cigars, he and I will be inseparable."

Mom was slim and stunning this evening, in a sleeveless royal-blue sheath that most women her age wouldn't have dared to wear. Her dark hair lay in a smooth shoulder-length bob, a sapphire ring sparkled on her right hand and her wit was as dry as ever. "So what did you get Carol for her birthday?" she asked, gesturing at the box under his arm.

"Uh...Turls got it. I'm not really sure what it is."

His mother shook her head at him. "But I'm sure the card is signed, 'All my love, Jack.'"

His mouth twisted and he shrugged.

"Don't you dare let them push you into it." Jeanne's voice was low, and she immediately turned toward another guest with her characteristic charm.

He knew exactly what she meant, cryptic as her words may have been. He moved farther into the capacious foyer of Henry Hilliard's stark-white, modern home on Star Island and shook the man's hand.

"Henry! How ya been? Looking good, my man."

The real estate baron slipped an arm around his shoulders. "Thank you, Jack. I've never been better." He eyed the wrapped box under his guest's arm. "A little big for an engagement ring, isn't it?"

"Ha, ha! Well, sir, I'm still trying to get up the nerve to ask you to marry me."

"Ha, ha, ha! Now *that* would send my daughter right over the edge." He slapped Jack between the shoulder blades just a little too hard. "She's in there somewhere, surrounded by admirers. Go find her, son."

Jack aimed a brilliant smile at Hilliard and got the hell away from him. The subtext of their conversation wasn't hard to figure out. If he'd been born into another culture and country, he'd be expected to offer a couple dozen camels for Carol's hand. Maybe throw in a few goats to seal the deal.

Truth to tell, he *had* meant to ask her to marry him by now. But that was before they'd slept together, and before he'd met Marly.

Jack stared at Carol, the statuesque blond goddess draped in demure, brown silk in the formal living room. She was gorgeous, a brown-eyed Grace Kelly. And she'd been like a sister to him since he was ten years old.

As if she could feel his gaze on her, she turned and raised an eyebrow. He crossed the room to her and kissed her on the cheek. "Happy birthday, Carol."

"Thank you, Jack." She glanced at a slim gold watch on her wrist. "I didn't think you were going to make it."

"You know I wouldn't miss your party." He extended the gift-wrapped box to her and watched her face carefully as she took it.

She rewarded him with a bland, delighted smile. "What's this?"

I don't have a flipping clue, honey. Jack shrugged and grinned. "It's a surprise."

"I just love surprises," she said.

No, you don't. You wanted something very specific from me for your birthday. But...I can't do it.

"Get yourself a drink, Jack." She signaled to a waiter in a tuxedo shirt and black bow tie. The boy came right over and offered a tray full of champagne flutes.

Jack took one even though he didn't feel like it. The last time he'd had champagne, he'd been in the limo with Marly. Naked. Sucking on her silver-painted toes, among other things.

"So, you ready to hit the campaign trail again?" Carol's eyes were beautifully made up with a gingery eyeliner and dark brown mascara. Her skin was flawless. Diamonds glowed in her perfect earlobes. Camera-ready Carol.

As if on cue, a photographer wandering through the party took a candid of them, both wearing switched-on smiles.

Was he ready for the grueling campaign? Jack grimaced. "Ready as I'll ever be."

The Carol he'd known at age ten had been skinny and sun-kissed with flyaway hair, a few freckles. She'd been fun. She could trounce him at tennis then and still could—if she hadn't turned into the kind of woman who would let him win just to save his ego. While Jack appreciated the thought, he didn't respect it. His ego was big enough without needing to win every game of tennis he played, thank you very much.

His ego was also big enough to handle Carol faking an orgasm the two times they'd slept together. She was a damn good actress emotionally—he'd give her that. But her body had told him another story, told him that she'd never let go for a second and had choreographed the whole thing.

She'd probably be extremely surprised that *he'd* faked his orgasm the second time. It was either that or lose his stiffie altogether. And though his ego was big, that was the one thing he didn't think he could handle.

So he'd tensed up and gasped like a landed fish, given a heartfelt groan and told her how amazing she was. Then he'd snatched off the condom and flushed it before she'd even left the bed.

His willie had wilted in peace without her discovering the truth: that her mechanical, preplanned seduction had failed miserably. And no matter how beautiful she was, he just didn't want to go there again.

As for marriage…Jack knew plenty of political couples who got together and stayed together for practical reasons. They made good roommates, didn't bother each other much, and threw great parties. They each traveled all the time campaigning, and created a highly successful, shiny business model.

As far as he could see, his parents' marriage had become that sort of union, though he didn't think it had started off that way. Somewhere along the line, though, Senator John had bonded with cigars, bourbon and golf while Jeanne had bonded with the kids. Senator John had done deals and written legislation while Jeanne had done diapers and helped write homework assignments. They cohabited.

It was a very civilized marriage, all in all. Nothing dramatic or tragic about it. But Jack just didn't think he wanted a similar arrangement. He wanted passion and abandon, shared laughter and shared meals.

He didn't have to be a rebel like his brother Tim—where was Tim tonight?—but he wanted a marriage that was more than a business arrangement.

The irony was that he was one hundred percent sure that Carol had seduced him in order to get things moving toward the altar. But her performance had had the opposite effect entirely. If he'd never slept with her he might be an engaged man right now. He might not have been free when he'd seen Marly's photo in *Shore* magazine.

"You don't sound so enthused about your reelection campaign, John-boy." Carol put his hand on her arm.

John-boy? Where the hell had that come from? Jack grimaced, hating the fact that she called him John. "Yeah, well, you know how it is. Relentless pressure, travel, public relations."

"I'm sure it gets lonely, too. You need someone to keep you company during the whole circus." She smiled sympathetically.

He gave her a noncommittal nod. "That's a lot to ask of someone, you know."

She raised her glass to her lips. "Well, the *someone* would have to care a lot about you and be strong enough to take on the load. Share it with you. And, like you, she'd have to look good while doing it. Make things seem effortless."

"Mmm." Jack resisted the temptation to drain his own glass and then go and bang his head against one of her father's stark-white walls. Major campaign contributor was Henry Hilliard. Huge. A guy didn't trifle with the man's daughter, or a guy might just have to find a couple of million elsewhere.

"Do you know who's the perfect, gracious, political wife? Laura Bush."

Jack had to agree with that. "Yes. She's beautiful, warm and unflappable in any social situation."

Carol nodded. "This is so funny, but the other day at the club a woman told me that I look just like a younger, blond, brown-eyed version of her. That was one of the nicest compliments I've ever been paid."

"You do, Carol. Of course, you're sexier." And he flashed a smile at her.

She dimpled, pleased. "Your father told me I looked like a delicious éclair."

Jack choked on a sip of champagne. "Did he?" *Was that before or after he pinched your lovely chocolate bottom?*

"He's got your charm, John, but none of your finesse."

Well, that tells me all I need to know, doesn't it? The before or after doesn't matter so much.

"Where is the old ja—uh, gent?" Jack asked, refusing to glower. "I should pay my respects." Or lack of them, as the case may be. His father had no business putting his hands on any part of Carol, especially when he was urging his elder son to marry her. The old goat.

"Last I saw him, he was outside debating the merits of various cigars with Jorge Martinez."

Oh, joy. I get to see both Pop and Martinez at the same time! Can the evening get any better?

"Is it true that your father's added an eight-hundred square foot annex to his home just to house a walk-in humidor and a wine cellar?"

"Yes," murmured Jack. "Carol, I'll find you again in a few. I'm going to say hello to the old man."

"Okay, John. But don't be a stranger." She kissed him on the cheek, and he was paroled.

He got another glass of champagne that he didn't want and moved through the crowd, greeting people he knew and meeting a few whom he didn't. It took him twenty minutes to get out to the verandah, where his loyalties were challenged immediately.

His father and Martinez were indeed hitting the bourbon and smoking cigars on one end of the porch. And on the other end lounged his little brother Tim, proud black sheep of the family.

Jack adored Timmy, in spite of his tattoos, the diamond stud in his nose and his tendency to rip the sleeves out of every shirt or jacket he owned. Tim wore black motorcycle boots in this heat, and stood with his arm around his drop-dead-gorgeous Brazilian girl-friend, who was wearing five-inch heels and a tiny ensemble that was probably illegal anywhere but Miami. It was a damned good thing that she grew her dark hair so long that it covered her ass, because Jack didn't think her skirt did the job too well.

He raised his hand in a two-fingered salute to Tim and Maya and then jerked his head toward Senior and Martinez. Without a word, his little bro understood that he'd find them as soon as he'd done his time with the old farts. Tim winked, and Jack headed over toward their father.

"There's my boy!" Senior's voice boomed. He clasped his son's hand briefly and then picked up his bourbon again.

Martinez shot Jack a medium oily grin.

Been talking about me, eh, Jorge? Jack returned it with a tight smile of his own.

"Goddamn, boy, your hair sure looks fine. Martinez tells me you've found a little gal in Coral Gables to do it," Senior said.

This time Jack didn't bother to rein in his displeasure. He glowered at Martinez. *You sonuvabitch.* To his father he said, "Yes, she's very talented."

"I'm sure. Though it might be more convenient if you went to someone in Tallahassee, don't you think?"

"Not really." Jack rocked back on his heels. "With my travel schedule, it doesn't make a hell of a lot of difference."

"I'm not sure you're getting my drift, boy."

"I'm getting your drift."

"Cigar?"

"No, thanks."

His father's eyes were the same as his, only blood-shot, with lines of hard living around them. The creases around Dad's eyes aimed down, while Jack's crow's-feet were laugh lines, aiming up.

"Visiting that salon in Coral Gables could get very expensive," Senior said.

"You're the one who taught me that a good haircut is everything in a campaign."

"Don't do it, Junior. It's extraordinarily bad timing."

Gosh, isn't everyone just full of advice tonight.

"Doesn't Carol look stunning?" His father gestured behind him with his cigar, managing to drop ash on the shoulder of his suit.

"Stunning," Jack agreed amiably, brushing it off for him. "You almost have to pinch…yourself…to make sure she's real."

Damn if his father didn't get bourbon down the wrong pipe. Jack swatted him on the back hard, in an effort to clear his lungs. Then he murmured his excuses and went off to join Tim and Maya. They were the only people here who would probably approve of him getting engaged to Marly Fine. And she'd need reinforcements within his family. Because sooner or later, like his great-great-grandfather before him, Jack was going to marry the woman whose picture had stopped him in his tracks and changed his life.

12

Sunday at 9:00 p.m. Marly awoke to the sound of her phone ringing. She opened her eyes and blinked, staring straight into the black, rectangular plastic dish that had held her dinner of grocery-store sushi. She'd fallen asleep in front of the television, sprawled over one of her big floor cushions. "Whah?"

Slowly her brain transferred the necessary commands to her arms and legs. *Get up. Wipe the drool from the corner of your mouth. Focus on the telephone. Punch the little button that says talk. Then follow that directive.*

She could do all of that. She stumbled to her feet and lunged for the phone. "'Lo?"

"Is this my favorite harem girl?" Jack's voice boomed into her ear.

"I don't think so." Marly pushed her hair out of her eyes. "At least, I wasn't aware of being part of a harem."

"You're not. Your apartment just reminds me of the *Arabian Nights.* You're the only girl I want in my harem."

"Oh," she said, still half-unconscious and unable to think of a witty comeback.

"Did I wake you? You wild party animal, you."

Marly frowned. "How did you get this number?"

"You gave it to me."

"No, I didn't."

He sighed. "Yeah, and frankly that hurts my feelings. You gave it to Mike! But anyway…I needed to get in touch with you and so I turned to the file."

"I believe that's cheating. It's also invasion of privacy and pretty obnoxious. Sir."

"Waking up cheerful, are we?"

"I'm serious, Jack." She yawned.

"Were you dreaming about me? Naked dreams, perhaps?"

"No." He'd never know she was lying through her teeth.

"Because I've been dreaming about you."

"Gosh, I hope that I've fulfilled your every fantasy—in your mind, anyway."

"Try to be nice, Marlena."

She shuddered. "Look, I'll be nice, but please don't ever call me Marlena. My mother calls me that."

"Sorry. So, I know that tomorrow is your day off and I was hoping—"

"Who told you that?"

"A little bird."

"A little blond bird named Shirlie?"

"I don't recall. Anyway, I was hoping that you'd allow me to send the Gulfstream for you, and you could join me up here in Tallahassee. How does that sound?"

"Jack—"

"I can promise you a really…explosive time. We

could send the entire staff away and run naked all through the governor's mansion."

She laughed at the image.

"And we could baby-oil the banister and enjoy sliding down it."

Now *that* sounded interesting.

"And in the morning, you could eat chocolate-frosted donuts off my erect—"

"Whoa. What do you mean, in the morning? Are you actually suggesting that you send the guber-jet for me *tonight*? You ever heard of giving a girl a little notice, Jack?"

"But I miss you," he said, like a little boy.

She decided to take a page out of Ms. Turlington's book. "Well, I miss you, too, *sir.*"

"Don't call me that. Turls calls me that."

"But I wouldn't ring you up in the middle of the night and suggest that you hop on the nearest flight to come satisfy my evil urges."

"I'm a big fan of spontaneity," Jack told her. "And I don't get to be spontaneous very often."

She sighed.

"Please come. If you come, you know you'll come a lot. We can spend the whole night together. I'm even the kind of guy who *snuggles*. I'm a dream come true."

"And what happens in the morning? Miss Turlington barges in to give us a sponge bath? Frick and Frack do a Cossack dance while serving us coffee?"

Choking noises came from his end of the line. "God!

You have quite the scary imagination. No, I promise that neither of those possibilities will occur."

If any other man had suggested that she fly to him in the middle of the night, she'd have told him in graphic detail what to do with his Gulfstream.

"Please come," Jack said again.

But this was the governor. And just talking to him was making her uncomfortably horny. The head of state wanted her to give him head in state. "When?" she finally asked.

"I can have a car at your apartment within an hour, and you'll be in the air half an hour after that."

"Okay." Was she easy, or what?

Jack gave a very undignified whoop. "I love ya, honey. Don't wear any underwear." And he hung up.

Marly stared at the phone. Had he just said that?

He had. But of course he didn't mean it.

Do you believe in love at first sight? he'd asked the day they'd met.

No. And neither do you. You are such a player, Jack Hammersmith. And you're great at it.

She only wished she didn't enjoy being played quite so much. She looked at the clock and figured she'd better get her butt into the shower, decide what to wear and pack.

THE GULFSTREAM was even nicer than the limo. The thing was decked out in shiny burled walnut, the way she'd seen on fancy yachts, and there was an actual sofa. The plane also sported its own monogrammed crystal, a bar, a sleep cabin with a bed and hardwood floors in the bathroom, which had an Italian glass bowl as a sink.

Marly just blinked at it all when Mike handed her into the thing and stowed her small duffel bag for her.

"How's the scrapbooking going?" she asked him.

He actually blushed. "Great. I'm working on my son's first year of preschool now."

She gave him the thumbs-up signal and he introduced her to Alan, the pilot. Alan was quite the laugh riot—he told her he'd only smoked a *little* crack that evening, but she had nothing to worry about.

She strapped herself in on the leather sofa, declined a drink and tried not to think about all the statistics on small plane crashes. She opened a *Vogue* magazine and stared at all the impossibly skinny models wearing impossibly expensive clothes. She thought again about the statistics on small plane crashes. She changed her mind about that drink and was on the way to Martiniville before they ever left the ground.

In about thirty seconds, they'd landed in Tallahassee and Alan helped her down the stairs with her bag. A different limo driver, Frank, drove her to the governor's mansion, where Jack skipped to the front door like a little kid to greet her. A very handsome, buff kid in suit trousers and a tie and shoes polished to such a shine that she could see her reflection in them.

"Welcome to the palace," he said with one of his disarming grins. Then he kissed her, right in front of Frank, whom he told in the nicest possible way to get lost. A fifty-dollar bill encouraged Frank to do so. Jack then turned his attentions back to her.

If she'd had panties on, they'd have melted. But she'd followed orders. Marly broke away from his kiss at a horrifying thought, though. "Are there security cameras in this place?"

Jack looked uncomfortable. "One or two."

"Out here?"

His sheepish expression answered her question.

"Then will you please take your hands off my ass?"

"Let me show you my personal quarters," Jack said diplomatically.

"That sounds great. Because I'd really rather not end up on the Internet doing nude acrobatics for a world-wide audience, courtesy of your fine security staff."

He shuddered. "I have to agree with you on that." He took her hand and her duffel and led her upstairs to his apartments in the big house.

Jack's taste ran to dark wood, Oriental rugs and rich fabrics. She looked around with delight, thinking that his preferences in interior design were a lot like hers— just more conservative and Republican—not to mention hideously expensive. But if he added floor pillows, candles and wall hangings and removed the lugubrious oil paintings of ducks…she could be quite at home here.

"You like it?" he asked.

"I do! And I didn't expect to."

"Why? You thought I'd have the place upholstered in gray flannel and pinstripes?"

She shook her head. "No, I thought it would look more like a hotel, with lots of gilded things and plastic flowers and stupid decorator objects."

"Stupid decorator objects?"

"Yeah, like those dumb balls made of grapevines sitting in bowls. What are those *for?* And old hatboxes that sit around in piles collecting dust. And books that are just there for display—God forbid anyone should pick them up and read them."

"And why would I have these objects in my personal space?"

"Because of your decorator."

"Ah. But I don't use one. I've had most of this stuff for a long time. And my mother ordered other things. She's the one who kind of pulled the place together."

He spoke of her with obvious affection, and Marly felt guilty that she didn't feel the same way about her mother. But then again, Mrs. Hammersmith probably had never made her son feel like an unwelcome intruder into his parents' relationship.

Marly turned and admired the high arched windows, the beautiful polished wood floors and the lush gardens she could see outside the window. "Do you have any pets?" she asked.

He joined her at the middle window and pointed toward a huge stone fountain. "Three koi. The biggest, fattest fish you've ever seen. One's white with orange speckles. One's solid coppery-orange. And one is this mustard-gold color with black splotches. They eat more than I do. I really expect them to do away with the gardener one day. They'll leave nothing left of him but hair and toenails."

"Ugh," said Marly. Then she brightened. "Maybe they'd like Fuzzy, my parents' cat."

"Poor little guy. What's he ever done to you?"

Marly put her hands on her hips. "You really want to know?" She told him about the portion of roast in the middle of her bed. "And when I went to take it away from him, he growled and snarled and hissed. You could see him trying to decide whether or not to lunge and bite me, or keep his fangs sunk into the meat so I couldn't take it away. Finally I flipped the comforter up over him and dragged him and the meat into the kitchen inside it. You should have heard him yelling!"

Jack said, "I didn't know cats could yell."

"Fuzzy can. So I shouted for my mother and she took one look and acted like I'd tortured him! Her poor little flesh-eating baby...she *let him keep the meat.* Unbelievable. She just laundered the quilt next day and cleaned up the mess on the floor, since he dragged that roast out of the kitchen and into the dining room, where he ate it under the table."

Jack was practically in convulsions. "You don't appear to think that justice was served, Marly."

"Go figure! My mother treats that cat better than she treats me. I'd throw him into a tank full of piranhas if I had the chance."

"No, you wouldn't."

She shrugged. "Okay, maybe not. But I sure do fantasize about it."

"Want a drink?"

"No thanks. I had a martini on the flight and that's enough."

"Want to join me in the whirlpool tub?"

"Now, that I might consider."

She followed him into a vast marble bathroom with a hexagonal tub. He shut the drain and turned gold taps on full-blast, while she admired the room. The gold had been done sparingly: just in the smaller fixtures. The towel bars were made of gleaming, rich wood, as was the architectural detailing and the double glass-paned door.

There were skylights in the ceiling and real plants grew in pots around the giant tub. There were several varieties of orchids, bromeliads and other flowering indoor plants she couldn't identify. If paradise could be achieved in a bathroom, this was it.

Jack smiled at her. "You like?"

She nodded. "You could hold a formal dinner in here, it's so big."

He rubbed at his chin. "I'll keep that in mind, honey. Though I find that the more naked people are, the more informal they get." He loosened his tie and started to remove it.

"Leave that on," suggested Marly with a wicked smile.

"Yeah?"

She nodded. "But take everything else off."

"You're giving orders very freely," he said, his eyebrows raised. But he didn't seem to mind, since he unbuttoned his shirt and obliged her.

Oh, that chest. The muscle in those shoulders and upper arms made her go weak.

"What about you?"

"You get to wonder if I followed *your* orders."

He cocked his head. "Mine are practically law. I mean, I am the head of state here. I could have you punished if you didn't adhere to my desires." His eyes gleamed and his teeth flashed white.

"Punished?" She tried not to laugh.

"Oh, yeah." Jack stood in front of her naked now, except for his signature royal-blue tie. Any other man would have looked utterly ridiculous. He looked as if he was about to do a photo shoot for *Vanity Fair. I'm ready for my close-up now, Ms. Leibovitz.*

"As I recall," he teased, "you caught my Republican part in Democratic territory last time, and threw him in jail without food or water. So if you break the Law of Jack, I should at least be able to spank you. I'm starting to have a really good master-to-slave-girl fantasy, here."

Outraged, she put her hands on her hips. "Master to—? You've got to be kidding me!"

He turned to shut off the taps before the tub overflowed, and she got a good visual of the Jack-Ass, smooth and muscular and beyond sexy. *Oh, my...*

He faced her again. "Are you talking back to the master, girl?" He stepped toward her, mock-menacing.

"Ye—uh, no!"

He grabbed her wrists and forced them—gently—behind her back, where he circled them easily with one hand. Because of the position, her breasts were thrust forward, which he didn't seem to mind a bit. He flicked her nipples with the thumb of his other hand, and her breath hitched in her throat, starting to come hard and fast.

Jack studied her for a long moment through his lashes, as if he liked what he saw, a lot. Then he brought his lips down hard on hers. His kiss sent shock waves through her and she melted under his mouth, opening to him and letting him take what he wanted.

When he lifted his head, she couldn't speak. Still holding her wrists captive, he traced his fingers over her lips, her jaw, down her neck and into her cleavage. She wished he would touch her breasts again, but he didn't. Instead he dragged his index finger down to her belly button and then lower.

"Did you follow orders?" he asked softly.

She'd never played sex games like this, and the experience was intriguing. What would he do?

"Did you, Marly?"

"No," she lied.

"Bad girl," he said. He tightened his grip on her wrists, looking stern and mock-menacing. "You know what we do with naughty girls like you?"

She shook her head, and her heart rate kicked up.

"We take down their panties and we spank them." He shot her a predatory grin.

Though the words and the concept were ridiculous, like something out of the fifties, they turned her on. She licked dry lips.

Jack stepped backward, hauling her with him, and

sat on the edge of the big marble tub. Then, chuckling, he forced her over his knee and pulled up her skirt.

I am so not doing this, Marly thought in shame. *This is laughable.* But as her midriff came into contact with his erection and cool air met her bare buttocks, electricity shot through her and she forgot all about dignity.

"So you did follow orders," Jack said, his tone pleased as he ran a hot palm over her bare rear end. But then he swatted her anyway.

Marly jerked her head up. "Hey!"

"You lied. There are consequences for that, too." He continued to fondle her backside, but now his fingers crept inward, along the cleft and lower down to—

She gasped as he traced up and down her sex, parted her and rubbed softly. Her breasts were squashed erotically against one hard, muscular thigh, and she got so wet she practically liquefied. Her body started to tremble and Jack shoved her thighs apart, then began to play her mons with his right hand like a musical instrument. Then, with his left, he began to touch and rub her nipples.

She felt helpless across his knees—literally like some slave girl. Whether it was the novelty of it, or the expertise of his fingers, or the faint suggestion of humiliation and powerlessness, Marly exploded into the most intense orgasm she'd ever had.

Jack lifted her and placed her gently on a rug there in the bathroom. She opened her eyes to find his blue ones boring into hers, that angel-devil blue on fire. He moved between her legs and she welcomed his hard, solid length into her body. The incongruous tie was still around his neck, and she grasped it and used it to pull his head down to hers. She kissed him like she'd kissed no other man before, thrusting with her tongue as he thrust into her. She let go the tie and clung to his shoulders, digging into all that gorgeous muscle and hanging on for dear life as his powerful body slid hers across the floor.

Unbelievable, but she felt herself building to climax again, and when he did that signature Jack circular motion with his hips, it triggered her into blissful oblivion at the same time he groaned out her name.

SINCE SHE FOUND IT impossible to move, Jack scooped her up again and got into the tub with her, settling them both down into the warm, silky water.

"You make one hell of a slave girl, kid," he said into her ear as he pulled her back against his chest.

"Do you have any idea how embarrassing that is?" She poked him.

"Why? It's just a fantasy. For all you know, I have dominatrix fantasies and want to be humiliated by an Amazon in a black rubber suit."

"Do you?"

"Well, no," he admitted. "I'd have her on her back in no time and get real creative with her whip."

She laughed. "So the black rubber thing doesn't bother you. The outfit has a few peek-a-boo holes, too, I bet."

"Oh, *yeah*."

"Well, master, we'll have to see what we can arrange." Marly turned her head and waggled her eyebrows at him.

"Oh, *maaaan*. See, I *knew* you were The One."

She froze. "Jack, you don't have to continue with that. I mean, you've already got me in your bed, or tub or whatever. You can quit with the BS."

His body stiffened behind her. "*What* did you say?"

13

JACK SPUN MARLY around. "You still think I'm feeding you lines. You think I'm a bullshit artist. Actually, you think I'm a liar. That's very flattering."

She opened and closed her mouth, her blue-green eyes wary. "I didn't say you were a liar—I just wanted to tell you that I know the score. Take the pressure off so you wouldn't have to keep up the…" Her voice faded out.

"Pretense? Yeah, I'm pretty sure that's the word you were going to use."

She looked away. "Jack, you can't expect me to believe in fairy tales."

"Sweetheart, you know by now that I'm no fairy. And I can assure you that I'm not telling tales. I have the cameo of my great-great-grandmother right out there in my dresser. You want to see it? You want to read the correspondence between her and the man she married, my great-great-grandfather?"

"Jack, I'm not trying to deny your family history! But things are different today, and I certainly don't expect—"

"A ring?"

She gave an embarrassed laugh.

"Why not? I *am* going to marry you, so you *should* expect a ring." Jack saw a shiver run through her, and then she just goggled at him as if he had three heads.

She threw up her hands, splashing them both in the process. "These are the kinds of things that you can't walk around saying or doing!"

"Why not? I just did." Jack leaned back against the side of the tub again, amused.

"Why not? Because…because maybe I don't want to marry you! Maybe it's just a little bit early in the game to be making sweeping statements like that. Maybe you're so sure of yourself that it's almost giving me the creeps!"

Jack folded his hands behind his head and got comfortable with the outraged, beautiful naked woman in his tub. "You sure are full of compliments. I'm a BS artist, a scheming manipulator and now I give you the creeps. You know, a guy with a lesser ego might take some of that the wrong way."

She stood, water sluicing down her body, and glared at him. Damn, she was one hot babe. He fixated on her breasts, that tiny waist, the beckoning patch between her thighs and those long, long legs. She was speaking, but he couldn't seem to register the words.

"That's just it! Your ego!"

Not worried at all about his ego, Jack fixated like a shark on a minnow. Then he honed in on his prey: the forbidden place right at eye level.

"You're so sure of yourself that it makes me want to—*ahhhhh!* What are you doing?"

Jack was licking. And holding her prisoner with one hand on each cheek, which he couldn't help squeezing.

Marly squirmed against him. "Stop that! You're not listening to a word I—*ohh.*" She clutched at his hair and swayed. "I said stop it!"

He ignored her as she started to pant and rock against him. He got down to the serious business of distracting her from whatever rant she'd been about to go on.

"*Don't* stop," Marly moaned.

Now that's more like it, thought Jack, pleased.

She whimpered. "Yes! Yes! Oh, please…"

He'd found the little nub at her center and he worried it with his tongue, making circles and figure eights. Suddenly she began to buck uncontrollably against him, while he held her hips in place. She made sounds that really weren't recognizable as words, little cries that told him he'd brought her ultimate pleasure.

It was only then that Jack got to his feet, stood her on the edge of the tub and drove inside her slick, tight heat. She lost her balance, grabbed at his shoulders and he took her weight completely. "Wrap your legs around me," he ordered.

She did, and he bent her back so that he could see her breasts, see their joining as he pulsed inside her. It was the sight of her, perpendicular to his body, laid out like a feast, that made him come in a hard, hot rush.

It wasn't until afterward, lying on the rug with her on top of him, that he thought of a condom.

"I'm on the pill," she told him. "And by the way, I may have no complaints at all about your technique, but that was a sneak attack!"

"Yup," he agreed, unperturbed.

"I was trying to tell you something important."

"I know." He grinned. "And I was trying to tell you something important, too. That I don't care what you say, or what barriers you erect, I'm going to get through them and I'm going to marry you."

"You act like I have no choice in the matter!"

He blinked. "You don't. Not really."

She gaped at him.

"It's fate," he explained. "Destiny. Whatever you want to call it."

The chills that she'd gotten the first time he'd said it to her returned. She didn't believe in fate. She believed in making her own destiny, whether or not it involved Jack.

And right now she believed in self-preservation, in not being swallowed whole by his outsize personality and calm plans for what was *her* life. "Fate," she scoffed. "You're crazy, Jack!"

He stroked her hair. "I love it when you get all hot and bothered. You're so damned cute."

"I'm not cute! And you're not listening to me." She sat up and glared at him.

"I am listening to you. Really. I'm letting you vent. I just don't happen to agree with you. You'll see that I'm right in the end. I'm always right."

"You—you—" She scrambled to her feet, angry and

naked. "You're such a—" She appeared to be search-ing for a word bad enough to describe him.

"Yes?"

"You're such a *man!*"

He pursed his lips. "It's true." He spread his hands apologetically. "I am a man. And *you* are a woman. And I think I'm about to hear you roar." He squinted, bracing himself.

She obliged, even though it was more of a shriek of frustration. She stalked out of the bathroom, leaving him on the rug.

He got up and followed. "I don't advise any more roaring, unless you want Jimmy and Rocket coming to see what's going on."

"Frick and Frack had better stay far, far away or I will bleach their hair while they sleep."

"Um," said Jack. "Rocket doesn't have any hair."

"Then I'll tattoo a pink poodle on his head."

"Beware the mad hairdresser." He walked to his highboy and opened the top drawer, pulling out a small silver box that had seen better days. He opened it and took out the antique cameo portrait, which nestled inside a gold locket. His great-great-grandmother's face looked up at him, eyes sparkling with mischief under her old-fashioned hairdo.

He walked with it over to Marly, who'd wrapped herself in his robe. "That's a little big on you. Here, take a look at this."

She turned away from the window and reluctantly took the locket from him. "So this is the lady who's caused all the fuss." Her mouth softened. "She's so pretty, Jack." She handed it back to him. "But she has nothing to do with me. You're turning a whim into destiny."

"I'm not," he said quietly. "Why don't you trust me?"

She threw up her hands. "Because you're a politician! A player! A Republican! What else can I say? You're glib, Jack. And you're too good-looking, too magnetic. One smile and people will give up their lives for you. I feel it working on me, too, and it scares the hell out of me. The impact you have on people is like nothing I've ever seen before.... You manipulate without even realizing it. Case in point—you just made me forget my own name, much less my argument about not being The One."

"I thought you said you had no complaints."

"I don't—except that you're asking me—no, *telling* me I'm going to marry you, and I don't have the slightest idea who you really are."

He shrugged. "I'm just me."

"What do you want out of life, besides to be governor? What do you do in your spare time? What movies do you love, and do you ever wish you could just throw your fifty royal-blue ties into the garbage?"

Marly stopped and drew breath. "And how do you know that I'm the perfect woman for you—The One, as you say? Apart from sexually?" She narrowed her eyes.

"Oh, that's right. You've got a whole file on me. But it won't tell you what my favorite foods are, or what music I listen to, or who I most admire in the world."

He nodded. "I understand. And I figure we've got all the time in the world to learn those things about each other. I didn't say I wanted you to marry me tomorrow."

She just folded her arms across her chest and stared at him, frustrated.

"Now, let me see if I can answer your questions. What do I want out of life, besides being governor? Well, first of all, I don't really want to be governor."

Her mouth opened. "You don't? Then why—"

"I was born into a political family, Marly. Born the son of a senator, and brought up around people who have a lot of influence—power, I guess you'd call it. I was set on a path from an early age, and I walked that path. I got rewarded with lots of positive affirmation, so I kept walking it. Before I knew it, the path defined me and developed momentum. It dumped me into law school, into my father's firm, and then into the political game. There are a lot of issues I care about, and I'm happy to be able to influence laws that deal with those issues…but I don't have to sit in the governor's seat to do it.

"What do I want out of life? Honestly? Just to be a regular guy for a while. Not be managed by campaign demands and PR demands. Not to be torn in a hundred different ways by the people who donate to my campaign and are lobbying for this, that and the other.

"I'd love, just for a few days, to be my little brother Tim. To dress like a rock star and adopt his screw-the-establishment attitude. But I don't have the luxury of doing that…. I have responsibilities to a lot of people.

Being governor isn't just holding the reins and yelling, 'Yah!'"

She remained quiet, just listening to him.

"It's endless meetings and speeches," he continued. "And documents and boring parties and public appearances. There are days when I'd rather have my balls waxed than attend another luncheon and make another canned speech that somebody else wrote for me."

He walked to his big bed and pulled the covers back. He patted the other side. "C'mere. You wanna talk? We'll talk." She looked so puzzled and lost in his big robe. The sleeves hung completely over her hands, and the hem trailed the floor as she joined him. He wanted to pick her up and hold her against him forever, breathe in the scent of her hair and wake up to those eyes every morning. Maybe he was crazy, as she accused him of being. But he knew in his bones that he wanted her next to him when they were eighty.

"So…then why are you running again, if your heart's not in it?" she asked.

"Babe, I'm running because we have momentum. I'm the incumbent. We have an agenda of change that we want to fulfill. I want to see the budget balanced. I want to see sweeping reforms on a lot of issues that I won't get into right now. The bottom line is that it doesn't much matter what I want personally—I owe it to my party, the voters, my campaign workers and contributors, even my family who has worked so hard to back me up. I owe it to them. So if I have to give up another four years of my life, I will. And no, it's not me trying to be noble. It's me…giving back somehow, taking the silver spoon out of my mouth and using it for some good."

Marly sat quietly, watching him with softened eyes. Good, he seemed to be getting somewhere with her. He pressed his advantage.

"Me running for reelection is a little like you dropping out of art school to pay off your father's medical bills. You put him over your own self-interest."

That hit home with her. He knew it by the way her pupils darkened, the way her lashes veiled them instantly, by her quick swallow.

He caressed her cheek with the backs of his fingers. "Do I ever want to burn my fifty royal-blue ties?" He chuckled. "You have no idea how much! I dream of putting one through the shredder, dissolving another in acid. I want to feed one to the disposal in the kitchen, flush another one down the toilet."

He dropped his head into his hands. "But the royal-blue tie is my signature, part of my public image. So I'll have to wait a little longer."

"Favorite movie?" she asked, settling back into his pillows.

"*Braveheart.* A tour de force. A masterpiece. Perfect in every way. It's a film that manages to be about courage and self-sacrifice and true nobility without descending into cheesiness. Very rare these days. How about you?"

She mused for a while. Then she nodded. "*Braveheart.* And *The Princess Bride,*" she added, pulling her knees up to her chin and hugging them. "It was so damned funny."

He nodded. "We'll have to rent that." He covered her hand with his and she didn't pull away. "Now, the only unanswered question, I believe, is what I do in my spare time. And here's the sad answer—I don't have any spare time. I actually made this time between us by canceling about three different social obligations."

"But if you had any?" she prompted.

"If I did, I'd...take guitar lessons. I'd make love to you a lot. I'd grow my hair long and grab you and a backpack and tour South America and Asia and maybe even hit the Australian outback. I'd go sailing every weekend."

"I don't know how to sail."

"I'd teach you." He reached over and tucked a stray lock of hair behind her ear. "So what do *you* do in your spare time?"

She looked at him sadly. "I don't have any, either. Not really. What I do have—my one day off—I usually spend doing laundry and cleaning and basically collapsing because I'm too tired to move. But I'd love to travel," she added in a wistful tone.

"Careful," he warned. "We're in danger of having a lot in common. We can't allow that, you know. Especially since according to you, I'm crazy and we're not getting married."

"I can't possibly have anything in common with a lowlife Republican," Marly teased. "I'm already violating all my principles by sleeping with a man who wears a suit and tie."

Jack lifted an eyebrow. "Funny. I didn't think you Democrats *had* any principles. Especially not Democrats with artistic leanings—ow! Don't make me call Jimmy and Rocket in here to defend me."

"Even Frick and Frack would admit that I had provocation for punching you." She shot him a sexy smile and he scooped her into his arms. "Hey! I can't have sex again. You've worn out all my parts. They hurt, you savage."

"Ah," Jack told her. "But I'm a tender-hearted savage. See, I can kiss them and make them all better…."

And he proceeded to do just that.

14

MARLY FELT as if she were living a dream as she fastened her seat belt again and accepted another martini in preparation for the flight back to Miami. What was she doing in Gulfstreams and limos, hanging out in the governor's mansion?

And had the man really announced that he was going to marry her one day? Why her? None of this made any sense. She was a hairstylist, for God's sake. She wasn't the kind of woman that heads of state wanted to marry.

She looked down at her loose, bohemian cotton dress and now-copper toenails. She tugged on her braid. She took another large swallow of her martini. The texture of the cotton and the smell of the leather couch, the taste of the gin and the roar of the Gulfstream's engines—all of these details told her that she wasn't dreaming.

Her body told her, too, since she could still almost feel Jack's hands on her, Jack's mouth on hers, Jack's rhythm inside her.

But wasn't she playing with fire? Could Jack swear his future over to her and the state of Florida at the same time? Wasn't she flying a bit high with this man? And if he had to choose…

Again, her common sense told her that he was too rich for her blood. His world was too exclusive, too different from hers, and things would never work between them.

Her mother's words during the atrocious dinner they'd shared in Fort Myers came back to her. *Probably not fancy enough for you…*

Well, she probably wasn't fancy enough for Jack, no matter what he said to her in the heat of desire.

God. What would Ma say if she could see her now? It didn't bear thinking about. Most mothers would be proud. Hers would be—

Marly almost swallowed whole the olive in her martini as a thought hit her. Her mother would be jealous. Was jealous. And she always had been.

The idea shocked her. Ma had been *jealous* all these years—of the attention and focus Marly got from her father, of the bond between them. And though it made her uncomfortable to think about it, she was afraid Ma envied her looks. Which was probably why Marly had never made a big deal out of them and didn't wear makeup.

As the jet carried her into the sky, her mind took her back over the years, fitting puzzle pieces together. Ma's impatience, her lack of encouragement on anything, her quiet fury when it had been Marly who saved her father's life by insisting he see a specialist.

Fury! Not relief or gratitude, but anger. Because

she'd been shown up by her daughter in the eyes of the man she loved.

She was competitive with her own daughter—not only for her father's love, but for a string of other things.

Ma had never had the chance to go to college. Ma had never been creative. Ma had never had her own business.

And what would her mother do if Marly became engaged to the governor?

She swallowed the rest of her martini and a small, awful, borderline-hysterical giggle escaped her. The scenario didn't bear thinking about.

The plane bucked a couple of wayward air currents, dropping suddenly and pulling Marly's stomach into the cargo hold. She gripped the metal armrest until her fingers turned white, half expecting to plunge downward through the clouds to her death.

Why couldn't she have died *before* she realized that her mother couldn't wish her well? Would never be able to wish her well?

She'd always carried inside a small flicker of hope that one day Ma would hug her to her bosom and tell her how proud she was of her. Tell her how much she loved her. Explain that all the years of nastiness had been due to some kind of evil spell that had now been broken by the miracle of maternal affection.

But that would happen when the winter Olympics commenced in Hell.

Ma wasn't evil or two-dimensional. She loved Fuzzy and she loved her husband.

She just can't love me. That's all there is to it. No big mystery, no unsolved riddle.

But tears filled Marly's eyes and rolled down her cheeks. One rolled right off the tip of her nose and plopped into the martini glass she still held on her lap. And then and there she made a promise.

If I ever have a child whom I cannot love, I will fake it to the end of my days.

Would she actually have Jack's baby one day? Marly tried to bend her mind around the concept, but it was so foreign. Could she be married to the governor and still have her own business? Run a salon?

And would their children go to Harvard...or to beauty school?

Another half-hysterical giggle slipped out of her mouth, and then another and another. Martinis and emotional turmoil and empty stomachs and high altitude sure didn't mix well.

At least the plane seemed steadier now, even if she wasn't. Marly unbuckled her seat belt and stumbled toward the Gulfstream's lavatory, where she sat on the floor in her funky cotton dress and cried while she giggled. She tugged at the roll of designer toilet paper on its little gold bar, pulling off half of it during the ridiculously short flight.

By the time they landed, she'd slapped sunglasses over her tomato-like face. She was arriving in style on a Gulfstream Jet, like some big-name celebrity. She might as well enjoy it and look the part, right?

Because no matter what Jack said and how much she might want to believe him, she was not The One and they weren't meant to be two.

THE FIRST PERSON Marly saw the next morning was Alejandro, who took one look at her and said, "Come with me." She followed him into the kitchenette, where he opened the freezer and took out a gel-filled eye mask. "Put this on," he ordered. "And then tell me all about it."

She sat in one of the wooden chairs, leaned back against the wall and did as he told her. "He's still insisting that he's going to marry me, Alejandro. That it's fate."

"He being Jack?"

She nodded.

"*Chica,* I must tell you that this is very non-Republican behavior."

She laughed. "I think I told him that. He doesn't care."

"What do you feel for this man, eh?"

"I don't know," she admitted. "Right now I'm back to thinking he needs a little white padded cell. But when I'm face-to-face with him..." She shook her head. "You've met him. You know how magnetic he is. When he stands there and looks into your eyes and tells you something with that sincere, blue gaze of his—all I can say is that you'd believe him, too. He's so charismatic. I swear he could put his hand on some woman's arm, tell her that she should step in front of a bus, and she'd smile back at him and *do* it. Gladly. With no regrets! She'd die happy because her last human interaction was with Jack Hammersmith."

"That is quite frightening, *mi corazón.*"

"You're telling me!" She slapped herself in the forehead. "You haven't even slept with the man."

"Nor do I wish to, if it's all the same to you."

She pulled off the eye-gel mask and met his eyes. "If he had been born gay and decided to convert you, you'd agree on the spot."

"No, I'm sorry. That's not possible."

"I'm telling you, it *is.*"

"No. There's a woman in my business school class…now for *her,* I would consider bouncing on my head to Boston. But your Governor Jack leaves me cold."

"Bouncing on your head to—" Marly stared at him and started to laugh. "My God, Alejandro, this sounds serious!"

He shrugged. "No. She doesn't know I'm alive. But she certainly is a concussion of a woman."

"A *concussion?* Should I ask?"

"No. Back to the governor," he said decisively. "So he can make people do what he wants. This is why he's in office, no? He has this skill."

She twisted her mouth. "Do you know that he doesn't even want to be in office?"

"Aha! This is a good thing. Because you would make a truly terrible first lady of Florida."

"Uh…thank you? You mean that as a compliment, right?"

"I mean it as a statement of fact. What would you do on the campaign trail, eh? Give free perms to all of Lake Okechobee?" His eyes twinkled.

"But, Alejandro, he's going to run anyway. So it's not a good thing at all that I would suck as a political wife."

"Ah." Her friend pursed his lips. "Then that is more difficult. You would perhaps have to sell out your interest in the salon to me and Peggy. You would have to get a makeover and change your clothing—"

"In other words, I'd have to become someone I'm not! And that's why this relationship between Jack and me will never work."

Alejandro folded his hands on the table. "I don't know what to tell you, Marly. You love this man?"

She blinked at him. "I—I—of course not. I don't know him well enough to love him."

"He says he loves you?"

She shook her head. "No. He says we'll get married, but he hasn't mentioned anything about love."

Alejandro looked thoughtful. "He is chasing you with a ring?"

"No. He's chased me with his great-great-grand-mother's cameo picture, but not a ring."

"So he has respect for tradition."

"Of course he does," she said impatiently. "He's a Republican. They're all about tradition."

Alejandro waggled a warning finger at her. "Stereo-types. But disregarding that, I've figured it out. He wants to court you the old-fashioned way."

Marly flushed as she thought about the very modern activities they'd engaged in recently. "Um, I don't think so."

"Trust me," Alejandro said with a knowing nod. "You'll be meeting his mother very soon."

"I WANT YOU TO MEET my mom," said Jack when he called.

Marly choked.

"What did you say?"

"Nothing." *I sure as hell don't want you to meet mine.*

"We'll be in Miami on Thursday on a fund-raising project," Jack told her. "Do you have any free time?"

Her heart sank. "I'm booked solid on Thursday. I'm sorry." She walked to the reception counter and bent over Shirlie's shoulder to see the appointment book. "I have a thirty-minute window for a meal between 3:30 and 4:00 p.m. That's it." Was that a little kernel of relief in her stomach? She really didn't know if she was up to meeting the governor's mother. There was no question that Mrs. Hammersmith would disapprove of her.

Jack stayed silent for a moment. "Well, if that's all you've got, then we'll take it. I'll arrange a reservation at Benito's, and we'll be there at three-thirty, okay?"

No. "Sounds great." *After all, it's not possible for your mother to disapprove of me more than my own does. So what's the harm?*

She tried to swallow her rising panic. Jack was introducing her to his mother, which meant that he really was serious.

Mrs. Hammersmith was going to take one look at her and flip out about the blue toenail polish—she was back to blue today—and the fact that she wasn't wearing a bra, and kept her hair in a braid. She'd object to her flip-flops and her three-inch-long silver earrings and her blue-collar background. Most of all, she'd hate what Marly did for a living and she wouldn't consider her good enough for her son.

"My mom," said Jack, "is going to love you."

Right. About as much as she probably loves to find rotting vegetables in the crisper. Except I'm sure she has a housekeeper and never opens her own refrigerator.

"I'm sure I'll love her, too," Marly managed to say. After all, she had a feeling it was socially incorrect to scream, "Don't bring your mother anywhere near me!"

"I miss you," Jack murmured into the phone.

"Me, too." And she did. She missed the person she'd been before she'd ever been featured in *Shore* magazine and gained a zillion clients and the passionate pursuit of the governor. She missed her uncomplicated prior life.

"Can't wait to see you. 'Bye, honey."

"'Bye." *Uh-huh. I need to tell him goodbye.* Preferably before she ever encountered Mama Hammer and her disapproval over the woman her son was nailing.

15

MARLY TOLD HERSELF that she couldn't break up with the governor over the phone. And she didn't have time to drive up to Tallahassee before he arrived. And without his help, she was fresh out of Gulfstreams to commandeer.

So here it was, Thursday at 3:37 p.m. and she'd broken out in a cold sweat waiting for Mike to steer the great white whale of a limo up to the door of After Hours.

"Have some class," Shirlie told her, snapping her gum. "Don't wait by the door like that. You're the queen. *They* are coming to *you*."

"I don't want to make a big ruckus in here," Marly said. "I want to be able to just slip out without anyone noticing."

"Well, at least step back here with me so you don't look like a dog waiting for its owner outside a grocery store."

Shirlie had a point. Marly joined her.

"Now, about the governor's package," Shirl whispered conspiratorially.

Thank God the phone rang just then. "After Hours, may I help you?" She dealt with the caller, making an appointment with Nicky.

Marly prayed for another call, but the stupid phone refused to ring.

"So, give me the goods." Shirlie fixed her with an avid gaze.

"Uh. You know how when you were little you pulled down your Ken doll's pants because you were curious? Well, it's like that. Nothing there. Nothing at all." Marly returned her gaze innocently.

"No!"

You have got to be kidding me. She's actually swallowing this? Marly nodded, keeping her face carefully blank.

"How can he not have a—? You're lying."

"Have I ever lied to you?"

Shirlie frowned. "I don't know." She thought about it. "But how can he not? How is that possible?"

Deadpan, Marly said, "I guess some people are just born without any genitalia. You know, like some babies have only three fingers, or end up a Siamese twin."

Shirlie's eyes were as big as dinner plates. "I guess *that's* why he's never been married."

Marly raised her hands, palms up, and shrugged. "I guess so."

Of course, Mike chose this precise moment to pull the limo up to the curb. She dashed for the door.

"Wow," mused Shirlie, still trying to get over the shock. "The governor has no... Hey! Wait! Then why are you dating him?"

"Power—haven't you heard it's an aphrodisiac?" Marly waved at her and let the door close. She doubled over laughing, though, and turned to watch the truth dawn on Shirl's face. She felt only a tiny pang of remorse, because it served the receptionist right for being so nosy. If *she* ever brought a boyfriend into After Hours, they were all going to rush the guy with calipers and a tape measure.

JACK'S MOTHER was statuesque, elegant and *warm*. Marly couldn't quite absorb this last, unexpected quality, but Mrs. Hammersmith appeared to be quite genuine as she took Marly's hand, covered it with her own, and said, "Aren't you lovely, my dear. Thank you for taking time out of your busy schedule to meet me."

She almost gaped at the woman. The wife of a former senator and the mother of the governor was thanking her, Marly Fine, hairdresser, for her time? *What's wrong with this picture?*

Moreover, Mrs. H. didn't blink once at her blue toenail polish or her lack of a bra or anything else. Nor did she turn a hair when Jack kissed Marly right there in the parking lot. All she did was ask, "Are you as hungry as I am?"

Marly suddenly realized that beneath all the anxiety, she was starving. So they trooped off to Benito's: Jack in his wing tips, his mother in her Ferragamo sling-backs and Marly in her rubber flip-flops.

"What about Mike?" she asked Jack. "Is he hungry?"

"I asked him, but he's got a sandwich and his scrap-booking. He came armed and dangerous with the glue-stick and everything." Jack's eyes twinkled.

Marly greeted Benito with a kiss to the cheek and watched, amused, as the little Italian bent low over Mrs. Hammersmith's hand and just about carried Jack in a litter to their table.

Heads turned all over the room, and she was relieved that Benito put them in a private room in the back of the restaurant.

Once they were all seated, Marly buried her face in the menu, even though she knew it by heart. Okay, so the governor's mom was a nice person. But what in the hell did she say to her?

I'm so glad you're not a witch?

Your son and I had tons of fun in the whirlpool tub a few nights ago. Would you like me to share the details?

So, who brainwashed you into being a Republican?

Marly had a feeling that none of these lines would be just right.

Jack began the conversation for her, addressing his mother. "I showed her the cameo, Mom."

Mrs. Hammersmith's hand stilled for an almost im-perceptible moment. Then she continued to empty a packet of sweetener into the iced tea Benito had brought for her personally. She stirred the tea with a long spoon, which she then laid beside her plate. She met his gaze, her eyes more gray than blue. "The cameo," she murmured. "I'd forgotten all about that."

She took a sip of her tea and then turned to Marly. "I understand now. Jack has had that locket for years, and he was always fascinated by the story behind it. When he was about twelve, he announced that one day he would do the same thing my great-grandfather did."

Jack smiled at her.

"And now he has—the only difference being that he didn't have to leave the country or learn Italian." Mrs. Hammersmith seemed to finish evaluating Marly in the course of another glance. "So, cheers! I think my son has made a wise choice."

Marly started to raise her glass, but then furrowed her brow and set it down on the table again. "Ma'am…excuse me for asking, but…how can you know that? You've only just met me."

Jack's mother nodded. "Yes. I've known you now for, what, five minutes? And during that time, you've told me far more about yourself than you realize. First, you didn't make anyone come in to get you. You came out to meet us, which was very thoughtful.

"Second, you didn't try to dress any differently than you normally do, correct? Which tells me you're secure in who you are. I like that.

"Third, you worried about Mike getting lunch. That was very kind. And you seem to have a warm, cordial relationship with the restaurant owner. I've noticed all of these things, as well as the fact that you don't use your looks. It doesn't occur to you that you could manipulate with your beauty, and you actually down-play it."

Once again, Marly was reduced to gaping at her.

"All of which informs me that you're a very nice girl and a rare find. Shall I go on?"

"I think you're embarrassing her, Mom." Jack touched Marly's arm lightly and then brushed his knuckles over her flushed cheek.

"All right. I'll say only one more thing. I also like the fact that you're skeptical about Jack."

Marly unstuck her tongue from the roof of her mouth. "How do you know I'm skeptical?"

Mrs. Hammersmith smiled at her. "You reveal it in the wary way you look at him, as if you can't quite believe he's there and might disappear at any moment."

Marly couldn't argue with that.

"I like you, young lady. But you two are going to have to make some hard decisions." She glanced at her son. "Jack, are you running again?"

His mouth tightened. Then he nodded. "Yeah."

"Things will be complicated. You can handle the media issues in one of two ways. Let me apologize in advance for being blunt, my dears, but either you need to lie low and not be seen in public together until after the election, or Marly is going to need a basic Stepford Wife makeover and a new job—preferably something on the campaign."

"What?" The four-letter word didn't even begin to express Marly's shock and distress.

Benito chose this moment to bustle in and ask them for their lunch orders, not seeming to notice the tension in the air.

They ordered salads and pasta, even though Marly had to get back to the salon in about fifteen minutes and probably wouldn't have time to eat hers.

Once he'd gone, she fixed Mrs. Hammersmith with an appalled stare. "Stepford Wife? Did I hear that correctly?"

Jack pinched the bridge of his nose between his thumb and index finger, while his mother gazed calmly back at her. "Yes, you did. Marly, I once dressed very much like you do now. It's a casual, comfortable look, but it won't do for a political wife."

"No offense to either of you, but *wife* is a four-letter word to me at the moment, and Jack and I have seen each other, what, four times? I think you might be jumping the gun, here. And what is this about me *quitting my job?*" Her mouth worked.

"Maybe we should order a bottle of wine and just relax and get to know each other," Jack suggested with a big, white smile. "We can have this discussion some other time."

"No," said Marly. "We have opened this can of worms, and I now want to see them all wiggling on the table."

He winced.

"Jack. I am…obviously attracted to you," she said, casting an apologetic glance at his mother. "In fact, I'm willing to admit that I could easily fall in love with you, even though you are a Republican." Was that a tiny snort of amusement from Mrs. H.?

"But I'm not Cinderella, and I don't even want to go to this—this—inaugural ball. I have a business, not a wicked stepmother. And I have business partners, not evil stepsisters. So I'm not interested in being rescued from my life, Prince Charming."

Jack lifted an eyebrow. "Well said."

Marly turned to Mrs. H. "And I could have sworn you just complimented me on not changing my *look* for you. So what's with the whole makeover suggestion?"

Jack's mother sighed. "I did say there were two different options. You can lie low."

"Why can't I just be me? What's wrong with my clothes? What's wrong with my job?"

"I like your look, dear. And your job doesn't bother me at all. But if you're in the public spotlight as Jack's girlfriend, fiancée or wife, the media won't be kind to a hairdresser with hippie tendencies. People are cruel."

"I don't really care what they say."

"You may not care what they say about *you*. But what about Jack and his goals? The media's attention needs to focus on him and his political platform, not on you and whether they think you're 'right' for him or not. You need to fade into the background, like most candidates' wives. I'm sorry, but that's the way it is." And in fact, Mrs. Hammersmith did say it in the nicest possible way, without malice of any kind. But her concern was obvious.

Marly took a deep breath. "I met Jack four weeks ago. Twenty-eight days later, you are asking me to go through a reincarnation as a different person?" Her voice rose on the last two words and she turned to him. "I can't believe you'd ask that of me. I'm not a toy, a doll. I'm not a tab that you insert into a slot. I'm a human being!"

He put his hand on hers, but she jerked away. "Marly. I'm not asking you to change. I don't even want you to change."

"But then understand," his mother repeated, "that you will have to lie low. You will have to be careful, or you'll be facing a media maelstrom." She clicked her French-manicured nails against her iced-tea glass, then caught herself and stopped.

God. I guess political wives aren't even allowed to fidget!

Marly pulled her napkin from her lap and tossed it on the table. "I'm not the right person for you, Jack. I've tried to tell you. I'm not cut out for your kind of life."

He leaned back, his jaw hardening. "Giving up that easily? I thought maybe you had some feelings for me. And I also thought you had more character, sweetheart."

She paused, wanting to scream and run out of there. "I don't think this is about character," she said quietly. "I think this is about you trying to twist me like a pretzel into something I'm not. Or keeping me swept under the rug like an embarrassment or a stain or a dust bunny."

"You're taking this the wrong way."

"How else am I supposed to take it?"

"Are you asking me to give up the throne, then, Wallis?" Jack steepled his hands on the tabletop. "Because that's what it amounts to."

She knew he referred to King Edward the Eighth abdicating the throne for his divorcée love, Wallis Simpson. "Why? Why does it have to be that way? Why can't the governor just date a hairstylist if he wants to? Is that just too lowbrow, too blue-collar, for Jack Hammersmith? Because I refuse to be ashamed of what I do for a living. I refuse to be ashamed of the fact that I am working class. And your average voter isn't sitting on a gigantic trust fund, either. So maybe dating a *peasant* could work in your favor!"

"Stop it, Marly," he said, his voice tight. "You know I'm not like that. You know my values aren't like that."

"Do I know it?" She stared at him. *The master and the slave girl, huh? That little fantasy cuts a bit too close to the bone.*

"Christ, I don't even *want* to run for reelection." He threw up his hands and turned his gaze on his mother. "You should run. I've said it before. You'd be a brilliant governor."

She laughed dryly.

"I'm not kidding," said Jack.

Mrs. Hammersmith began to twist her wedding bands, and then stopped, caught fidgeting again.

"You ran our household like a well-oiled machine. You could run the state with your eyes closed."

"Don't be ridiculous."

"You speak fluent Spanish and would be perfect to liaise with Latin America...whereas I stumble through the language with a crutch and a pocket dictionary and a phonetic teleprompter."

Benito danced in with a tray holding their salads and put an end to the conversation. Marly put her napkin back in her lap, intrigued by the new topic.

"Fresh pepper? Parmesan for the Caesar?" When he'd tended to everyone's needs, he disappeared again.

"You have a law degree," Jack said to his mother. "You have all the connections I have, and you've been instrumental in the campaigns—both Dad's and mine. What's stopping you?"

"We're straying from the subject," said Mrs. H. briskly.

He gave a good-natured laugh and shook a finger at her. "No, we're straying from *your* subject. We're talking about spin—what could be better spin than *Working Mom Runs the State?*"

Marly chimed in. "Oh, I like that!"

"This restaurant is very nice," Jack's mother said, ignoring them both with a charming smile.

"Is it Dad who's stopping you?" Jack asked.

She put down her fork. "No. It's my son, the incumbent and the stronger candidate. Keep in mind that this isn't only about you or me. It's about what's good for the party. Now, how's your salad?"

"Just peachy."

Marly glanced at her watch and realized that she was already two minutes late for her next client. "I'm so sorry, Mrs. Hammersmith, but I've got to get back to After Hours. I have a customer waiting."

Jack's mom nodded. "That's all right. And I do apologize if I upset you, Marly. I've just been in this racket for a long, long time. Please believe that I only have your best interests at heart."

Marly extended her hand. "I know that. Thank you. Jack and I...have some things to discuss."

He stood up politely as she rose—his manners had been bred into him from the time he could crawl. It was one of the things she loved about him, but also one of the things that made her conscious of all the differences between their backgrounds.

She wondered what Jack would do if he ever faced her mother's noodle surprise. It was a far cry from lobster ravioli. Or her roast? He'd probably hand-carry it for Fuzzy to the center of the guest bed and lay it on a napkin for him. Maybe he'd even say grace.

Dad would think Jack was a smooth, smarmy politician and Ma would be struck mute, strangled by sour grapes but mesmerized by his looks.

"It was very nice to meet you, Mrs. Hammersmith. Enjoy your lunch—and if you're ever in the neighborhood and need a haircut, come see me." Marly smiled at her and walked to the door. Then she turned and added, "And by the way, I'm a pretty good judge of character, too, and I think you'd make a fabulous governor."

16

MARLY POKED at the dry, icky sushi pieces in the plastic takeout container in front of her. The cooked imitation crab in the center of the rolls didn't look in the least bit appetizing.

She sat on one of her oversize cushions opposite Peggy, who'd come over for a glass of wine and who looked equally unimpressed with the sushi.

"How can you eat that stuff?" Peggy asked with a shudder. "Raw fish…*eeeuuww.*"

"This contains no raw fish," Marly said. "And besides, when it's really fresh, spicy tuna or salmon or eel is to die for."

"Yeah." Peggy took a sip of her wine. "To die for, writhing in pain with food poisoning or a vicious attack from some microbial organism."

Marly rolled her eyes and changed the subject. "So, Troy is in New York, you said?"

Her friend nodded. "Putting in orders for the new sporting goods store. He's been so excited about it, like he's planning Christmas morning for an entire city or something." She grinned. "It's the first time he's ever gotten to control his future one hundred percent. As a football player and then as a coach, he was always answering to someone else and could be traded or fired on a whim."

Marly nodded and put the lid back on her tray of sushi. She just wasn't hungry. "What I don't get, Peg, is how your love life is going so well after you stranded the guy naked in the After Hours mud bath!"

Her friend stared into her wineglass sheepishly. "Well, though I thought I was pretty clever at the time, you know it wasn't my proudest moment. Let's just agree to forget that, okay? Tell me what's going on with Governor Jack."

Marly grimaced, got up and stuck the sushi in her refrigerator. She came back into the living room with the other half bottle of chardonnay and plunked it down on the floor in front of them.

"Governor Jack is a trip. He's funny, he's hot, it's the best sex of my entire life—yes, including Arnie-the-drummer-from-the-band-that-will-remain-nameless."

Peg's eyes widened. "You're having the best sex of your life with a Suit? And a *Republican*?"

Marly nodded, tongue-in-cheek. "Yeah, can you believe it?"

"So where do you think this is all headed?"

"If he has his way, it's headed toward me in a twin-set with a fat pink bow on my head, gazing adoringly at him in front of a sea of people." Marly pulled a floor pillow toward her, flopped onto her stomach and shuddered.

"Fat pink bow…no! What, you're going to be his Betty Boop on the campaign trail? I forbid you."

"You'd better get ready to alligator-wrestle his mama, then. She's got it all worked out."

Peg's expression became militant. "Ve haf vays of dealink vith Evil Mothers. Troy can kidnap her, I'll give her sciatica and you zap her with the poodle perm. Maybe overpluck her eyebrows and dye them orange, too."

"But she's not evil," Marly wailed. "She's very nice. She was just being realistic. If the media finds out Jack and I are an item, the shit will hit the fan. It calls attention to his bachelor status and morals, plus it takes the focus off him and his leadership skills and puts it on me, the *hippie hairdresser.*"

Peg stared at her. "Oh, I get it. Sex with a bow-head is more moral?"

"Well, I'd look sweeter under a bow or a velvet headband. More proper and wholesome."

"Marly, that's the most ridiculous thing I've ever heard."

"Well, the alternative to the twin-set and bow is to be the Top Secret Slut-Behind-the-Scenes. Does that play better, when it comes out?"

"Maybe you should find another boyfriend. This sounds like a lose-lose situation."

"That's what I'm thinking. Maybe a nice, low-key fertilizer salesman or John Deere rep."

"Go with John Deere. Wasn't that guy who murdered his wife and unborn child in fertilizer sales?"

"Good point."

Peg poured herself some more wine. "You?"

Marly shook her head. "No. I've got to figure out exactly what I'm going to say when I break up with Jack. And I've got to do it soon, because there are already little sound bites on the news about him gearing up for the campaign trail, and whether or not the Democrats will have a strong enough candidate to beat him."

"I don't want to drive home," Peg said, looking sleepy and comfortable. "Can I sleep over tonight?"

"Sure. You can help me rehearse."

MARLY TOSSED AND TURNED all night in her bed, got up several times and stared with envy at Peg, who was gently snoring away on the floor in her living room. Then she went back to the bedroom and thrashed around some more, visions of Jack swimming through her mind.

We need to talk. It's not you, it's me. You're a very special person, but...

I think we should see other people. I love you but I'm not in love with you. We just don't have anything in common. I don't think I can give you what you need....

All of these lines had been running through Marly's head for hours when the phone by her bed rang the next morning. "Hello?"

"You're going to break up with me, aren't you?" Jack's voice spoke into her ear.

"What?" she said, appalled. "Uh...no! Why would you think that?" *I'm going to kill you for blindsiding me*

*like this! All night I rehearse, and you catch me off
guard?*

"I put myself into your cute little rubber flip-flops,
Marly. I tried to choose between being transformed
into a Stepford Wife or being swept under the rug like
a shameful secret, and neither appealed to me very
much. I thought, 'Hey, it's easier to get rid of the pesky
guy, even if he's handsome, charming and great in
bed.'"

"Modest, too," she couldn't resist adding.

"Mmm. So I said to myself, I said, 'Jack, dude. She
doesn't want your money, she's not the single-strand-of-
pearls type, and—though it's tough for a man to admit—
there are bigger penises out there. She's going to ditch
you and wash her hands of the problem.' Am I right?"

It's not you, it's me. "Why—why would you think
that?"

"I just told you," he said patiently. "So here's the
deal. You're not going to sing my swan song until we've
had a chance to see each other again and talk."

"I'm not?" Marly was nonplussed. "I mean, no, of
course not! I had no plans to…" *God, could you just
make a cup of coffee appear magically in my hand?
This is so unfair!*

"I'll get down there as soon as I can, okay? And you
have to promise to hear me out. I have to warn you, I
can be very persuasive."

*Like I didn't know that already? As if I'd normally
end up in bed with a nut who picked my photo out of a
magazine and fixated on me in a totally unhealthy way?*

"Jack, like I said, I don't know where this is coming from—"

He chuckled in her ear. "Save it, honey. You're not as good at snowing people as I am. I've had years of experience."

She held the phone away from her ear and stared at it, almost shrieking in frustration. He was several steps beyond intuitive—in fact, he was almost creepy. Was Jack Hammersmith the first *psychic* Republican governor?

"So I'll see you soon, okay?" he said. "Promise you'll think about me. And don't wear any underwear." This sentence was followed by a dial tone.

Marly clutched the phone for a long moment, staring at it, and then banged it against her forehead. Heat bloomed all over her body and someone—gee, who?—had flipped the On switch to her erogenous zones.

How could she want to sleep with him and murder him in the same exact instant? What was wrong with her?

Maybe it truly is me, not you....

THE FABULOUS FOUR, fresh from an expedition to Miracle Mile, brought all their shopping bags into the salon with them to show off their new duds. And, to Marly's horror, Denise brought a bag of cheese popcorn and a chilled ring of shrimp with cocktail sauce in the middle.

Within forty-five minutes, they'd finished off two bottles of chardonnay and created utter chaos inside

After Hours. Marly came out from the back to find Suzette *standing* in the chair at her station, modeling a clingy, new Herve Leger dress and shaking her booty for Nicky, who applauded.

Denise had draped three other outfits over Nicky's chair and swayed slightly as she asked everyone in earnest whether she could still get away with wearing a chartreuse micromini at her age.

Marly squinted at it, the color giving her a headache. But since Denise had had about fifteen years surgically removed from her body, she allowed faintly that yes, Denise could get away with it.

Marly helped Suzette down from her chair before she fell and impaled herself on a hot curling iron. But she turned to find Rebecca with five shoe boxes open all over the pedicure area, twinkling her toes in a pair of $795.00 Sigerson-Morrison stilettos. Dear God, if there was the tiniest puddle and she slipped, lost her balance...

"Alejandro!" she called. *I need you to lock up these women.* "Come and see the fashion show, sweetie."

He must have recognized a note of panic in her voice, because he emerged from the spa's office right away and moved in masterfully to dance Rebecca out of danger, compliment her new shoes and whip them off of her so he could wrestle her into a pedicure chair.

"But, darling," she said with a giggle and another slurp of wine, "I don't need a pedicure. I just had one two days ago."

Alejandro picked up one of her feet and smoothed a big hand over it. "They are a little dry, *mi corazón*."

She appeared to slip into a coma at his touch—most women did. Then she picked up her glass again and purred, "Whatever you say, Señor Manos."

It was his least favorite nickname, but Alejandro smiled stiffly and began filling the pedicure basin with warm, scented, bubbly water.

Marly bit her lip to keep from laughing. Looked as if the White Knight was going to be pushing back her cuticles for a while.

The fourth of the Fab Four, Natasha, was focused almost entirely on the shrimp and cheese popcorn, which made things really hard on her manicurist. A wilted popcorn blossom floated in her soak bowl, and a shrimp tail swam among the nail polishes to the right on her table.

Natasha had also found an ingenious solution to the problem of how to drink wine while getting a manicure: a straw emerged from her glass.

If this hadn't been going on in *their* salon, Marly would have found the whole situation funny. She exchanged a helpless glance with Alejandro as she exclaimed over the ladies' fashion finds.

She, Peggy and Alejandro had marketed After Hours as a preparty hot spot for beauty treatments…so they had to put up with a little partying. No way around it. But jeez! All they needed at this point was for a bunch of guys to meet every week for poker and massage.

"Bite your tongues!" hissed Peggy when they said this to her. Then she assumed a thoughtful expression. "But if Marly keeps dating Jack, soon we might be hosting legislative sessions here, with three-martini lunches."

Marly is not going to keep dating Jack, no matter what he says. No way was she welcoming a herd of senators and their aides into the spa. Her imagination ran away with her and she imagined a week-long filibuster....

As the Fab Four consumed another two bottles of wine over the next two hours and scattered smelly shrimp tails all over the place, she forced herself to focus on the fun salsa music and her clients' hair. Just ignore them...but she couldn't help worrying. It was getting late and the Fab Four's car keys needed to disappear before one of them decided that driving was a great idea.

Peggy had gone home, Nicky got off at eleven, and she and Alejandro were due to close together. One of them counted out the registers while the other cleaned up.

A whispered conversation with Nicky revealed that he had a date, so he couldn't stay. Marly decided to go ahead and call a cab for the ladies. When it arrived, they'd shepherd them into it with all their shopping bags; they could pick up their cars in the morning after sleeping off their hangovers.

But when the cab got there, confusion reigned. "I didn't call a cab," said Rebecca, sounding affronted. "I'm fine to drive. Did you call a cab, Natasha?"

Natasha answered in the negative. "Suzette?"

Nope. And Denise hadn't, either.

"We don't want a cab," they announced in unison. "Send it away."

Great. Now what do we do? Marly and Alejandro exchanged another glance. He stepped to the plate.

"Ladies," he said, "I have fallen in love with you all. Please allow me to take you home. I'll be heartbroken if you refuse."

They giggled. "But we all live in different homes," Denise said, gazing up at him from under her lashes. "Which one of us do you want?"

"All of you," he said again.

Suzette's eyes widened. "Are you suggesting…?"

"No!" Alejandro looked alarmed. "No, no. That would be to disrespect you."

"Bummer," said Rebecca. "I'm kinda partial to being disrespected, at least in the bedroom."

Natasha elbowed her. "But we're not ready to go home yet, anyway. Our husbands are on a hunting trip. We want to go to South Beach and party!"

"Yeah!"

"Yeah!"

"Will you take us?"

Alejandro's mouth worked. "Ladies, I don't think—"

"You're almost done here anyway, and we've seen you dance. C'mon, big guy! Let's *paaaaaarty!*" They all whooped and hollered and jumped up and down.

"Looks like I'll be closing by myself," Marly said, her voice dry.

SHE WAS PUSHING piles of chopped hair around with a broom when Jack showed up and knocked on the locked door. His suit was immaculate, but he'd loosened the blue tie and the limo was nowhere in sight. Dark circles had settled under his eyes and he sported a five o'clock shadow over the lower half of his face.

She wasn't sure she could handle breaking up with the governor right now, not after this day from hell. She felt like sending him to South Beach to party with the not-so-Fabulous Four. Marly leaned on her broom and stared at him. What was he doing here at such a late hour, anyway?

He raised his eyebrows and gestured at the door, clearly saying, "How'd you like to let me in?"

God. If only she didn't know what he looked like naked under that suit. Because the problem with letting Jack in was that he could get her from zero to sixty sexually within three seconds. And then she'd really let Jack in, so to speak. In and out, and in and out, and in and out.

Her body was ready for him by the time she reached the damn door, and his tongue was in her mouth before she had it open more than a foot. His hands were up her shirt and his knee was between her thighs and she was charged with electricity and crackling under his touch.

She wasn't sure how, but she had the presence of mind to lock the door again once they were inside. She tried to force herself to remember all those breakup lines she'd gone over in her head, but with Jack's lips on hers it wasn't easy.

We need to talk.

But first, let's make love over and over and over again.

It's not you, it's me.

So not true! We both lunged at each other.

I don't think I can give you what you need....

Give it to me, baby! Give it to me now.

I think we should see other people....

Oh, God. There are other people! Outside the window! People with cameras and flashes and long, skinny notepads. *Reporters are swarming After Hours like flies and our hands are up under each other's shirts!*

17

HORRIFIED, Marly broke away from Jack and dashed for the drapes. She pulled them with one hand and shielded her eyes from the flashbulbs with the other, while he swore a blue streak and snatched his discarded jacket from the floor.

Fists pounded on the door of the spa, which was clear glass and didn't obstruct the view at all. A blur of jostling heads and lenses and suits appeared there.

They could hear shouted questions. "Governor, how long have you been dating the hairstylist?" "Jack, what do you think Carol Hilliard will have to say about this?" "Governor, how do you think this will impact your chances for reelection?"

"Goddamn it!" Jack exploded as they ran to the back room and closed the door. At the front desk, the phone started ringing.

"Marly, I'm so sorry. I didn't see anyone tail me here. I didn't take the limo because I didn't want to attract attention, and they still got me."

She tried to get control over her breathing, but it was difficult. The shock of having her privacy invaded, having people screaming at them through the windows—it rattled her. She shook with adrenaline and her palms poured sweat. She blinked rapidly, which made everything seem as though it were occurring under a strobe light.

"Those pictures… Jack, I don't have to tell you that they're not going to be flattering."

He closed his eyes and slumped against the wall. "No, they won't. Jesus, I had my hands up your—and I was, um, visibly turned on. I'll have to alert Martinez and Lyons, get them prepared. And we'll have to figure out how to spin this. I'll need to get you some security…."

She gulped for more air. "Surely not? Those reporters can't come into our place of business, can they?"

"Honey, you can ask them to leave, but that is a city sidewalk out there and you have a glass door. They can film and harass every employee and client who comes in here." He thought for a moment. "I'll have somebody get butcher paper over here so you can cover the door."

She stared at him hopelessly, still trying to regulate her breathing. "This is what your mother was talking about."

He nodded soberly.

"How long are they going to camp out there in front of the door?"

He didn't answer, just twisted his mouth.

"They can't stay there all night!"

"Oh, yes they can."

"But—how are we going to get out of here?" She looked wildly in the direction of the back door, but he shook his head.

"Trust me, they've already got people staked out there, too."

"Jack! We can't sleep here—the couches are in the front room near the door. And the only other comfortable option is my partner Peggy's massage table."

He put a hand on her shoulder. "We won't have to sleep here, but we're stuck for a little while. I'm sorry. I really am." Inside his trouser pocket, his cell phone began to ring. Jack pulled it out and answered it. "Yeah, Martinez. We've got a regular shit-storm outside. Reporters are hurling themselves against the windows like the zombies in *Shawn of the Dead*."

Under any other circumstances, Marly might have laughed at that. Not now.

He winced. "Yeah, I know. We're locked inside the building but it's not exactly comfortable. You think I should give 'em a statement?

"No? Okay. Martinez, you know what? I don't need to hear that right now. What I need is a security detail to get us out of here." He listened for a moment, then flushed with embarrassment. "Yeah, no," he muttered. "I sent Jimmy and Rocket to the store for a bottle of champagne." Jack held the phone away from his ear. "Look, it's done now. They'll probably arrive any minute. Fine. Goodbye."

Marly took the end of his tie and slipped it through her fingers. "You ditched Frick and Frack for me?"

Jack moistened his lips, staring down at her. He cupped her chin. "Uh-huh."

"Because you knew they bothered me?"

He nodded. "And I just wanted a little bit of alone time with you."

"That was sweet, Jack, but you could have been putting yourself in danger. Don't ever do that again."

"What I'm afraid of is that I put you in danger. I had no idea anybody was on to us."

She didn't remind him that he'd kissed her publicly on at least two occasions, and anyone who'd seen them could have passed on the word.

"Me in danger? I'm just a hairdresser. That's silly. But this is a mess." She tugged on his tie. "They're going to say you have poor judgment, and that I'm some low-class slut—"

"Sh." He put a finger over her lips. "I won't let them say that. And I've never had better judgment than the day I—fixated on you."

"Fixated. That's an odd word choice."

"Marly, sweetheart. You got upset when I mentioned love at first sight. You want me to say, 'the day I fell in love with you'?"

There he goes again. He's got to be the most stubborn, misguided guy in the state—which is just what the media would say if they had a clue about any of this.

"You didn't fall in love with me, you fell in love with a picture."

Jack put a finger over her lips and tugged gently on her braid. "Hey, we're not going off on that tangent again. You're more comfortable with the word *fixated*, because it's easier to criticize and disbelieve. You can't argue with love, really. It's mysterious and unexplainable and one person cannot tell another person that he or she doesn't feel it."

She stuck out her chin. "Can, too."

Jack settled the argument with a deep, sensual takeover of her mouth. He spanned her waist with his hands, caressed her breasts lightly with his fingertips, and managed to wipe her mind blank of anything but him and his scent—Gray Flannel and aftershave and just Jack.

"So let me show you just how fixated I am on you…" Before she knew it he'd lifted her up and set her on Peggy's massage table, rucking up her skirt to her knees.

She tore her mouth from his. "Jack, we can't! There's a pack of wolves howling out there, and Frick and Frack will show up any moment and—"

His mouth descended over hers again and he ate the end of her sentence. Her body lit like a human torch and she gave in to desire. He stroked the back of her neck, nibbled at her ears and circled her nipples with his thumbs. He stood inside her spread thighs, shoved his hands up under her cotton shirt, commandeered her breasts and reduced her to a whimpering puddle of need. He suckled them, licked them, nipped them with his teeth.

Without even being conscious of it, she reached forward between his legs, found his erection and squeezed.

Jack cursed softly as she unzipped his fly, pushed layers of fabric away from his cock and caressed it in her palm. She shrugged off his hands on her shoulders, slid off the massage table, knelt and took him into her mouth.

Jack reeled and had to steady himself as she rolled her tongue down the length of him, sliding over the soft skin easily. She closed her lips around him and sucked.

It seemed there was only so much Jack could take. Gasping, he pulled her up by the shoulders and practically threw her back on the massage table with her skirt around her waist. Pulling her panties to the side, he hauled her to the edge of the bed and plunged into her again and again.

She came almost at once, excited by the sheer need he seemed to have for her and the sight of him out of control. He might be trapped in a suit and tie all day, but he was not quite civilized underneath.

Jack was overwhelming in a hundred different ways and made her forget everything but him. She forgot about the media shit-storm raging outside, and her worries about how this would affect her career, and the salon, about what her parents would think....

All she could focus on was him filling her, over and over like a well-oiled piston, the look of intensity in his eyes, of primal connection, shattering her control.

She arched against him helplessly as he stroked her breasts and toyed with her nipples. Eight inches of Jack streaked across her clitoris and she dissolved **into bliss yet again.**

He gripped her bottom, digging his fingers almost painfully into her flesh, and impaled her one last time, his own back arching. He ground his pelvis into hers and spilled into her with a groan—just as his cell phone began shrieking again.

He slumped over her, pressing his cheek to hers, and she felt their hearts pounding in sync.

The cell phone stopped and then started ringing again.

"You'd better answer it," she whispered into his ear. "It's not like they don't know where you are." She handed him a towel from the pillow next to her, and he pulled out with a sigh.

But he leaned forward and kissed her deeply, possessively and thoroughly. "You're not breaking up with me," he said. "You got that?"

She stared at him, at his loose tie and rumpled hair and crushed shirt. His blue eyes burned into hers and she still lay open to him, in the most vulnerable position. Her heart turned over.

And then Jack Hammersmith, governor of the state, said the most peculiar thing. "I need you, Marly. You're it for me. Perfect in every way." Stunned, she didn't know what to say.

Finally, with pants zipped and shirt tucked back in, he answered the phone in clipped, efficient sentences. Marly sat up and straightened her own clothes, still wobbly from his touch. When he hung up, he said to her, "They're on their way to pick us up, but there's no way we're getting past the phalanx of cameras out there without them taking more shots. You're either going to want to smile and stand proud, or use something to cover your face."

"Yeah…I can make a space helmet out of one of the stationary blow-dryers."

Jack's lips twitched. "Add some aluminum foil antennae, maybe? Paint your face green."

"And tell 'em I've been taken *by* their leader, over and over again?"

He cracked up. "See, you're perfect."

"I'm not," she insisted. "I'm a Democrat. You're a Republican."

"You show me the other side," he said, leaning against the wall. "Next argument."

"I'm blue collar. You're blue blood."

Jack snorted. "Blue blood? Hardly. My ancestors came to this country without two cents to rub together. You'll have to do better than that, honey."

"I drive around in a Mitsubishi. You travel by limo and private jet."

"Tell you what, Jimmy and Rocket will love being squashed in the back of a compact." He grinned. "You give me your keys, and I'll give you Mike and Alan. Or better yet, you can just travel around with me."

"And what would I do while you're running the state?"

"Paint," he said promptly. "Draw. Design things."

That shut her up.

"You could do that for four years…and afterward do anything you want."

His phone rang again. Jack sighed and flipped it open. "Yeah. Okay. Thanks. We'll go out the back door." He flipped it closed.

"Frick and Frack, as you call them, are out back. The limo and more security will be here in about two minutes. You need to decide where you want to go— they're suggesting you don't go back to your apartment, though, since the media has dug up your address."

"Oh, God." She put her hands to her face.

"You want to come back to Tallahassee with me?"

"How would I get to work in the morning?"

Jack put a hand on her shoulder. "I don't advise you to go back to After Hours for a couple of days. It'll be rough."

"It's my job! I'm fully booked. I can't just let down my clients like that."

"Again, Marly, I'm sorry. But this is a little bigger than trims and highlights."

Was his tone just a little patronizing? She couldn't be sure—she was too upset to catch subtleties at the moment.

"So what do you want to do?"

"Take me to Alejandro's. He's not there, but I know where he keeps a spare key."

"Who's Alejandro?" Jack's voice tightened.

"My husband."

"Your *what?!*"

"Kidding, dude. Alejandro is my business partner and friend. You've met him. I've known him since I was ten."

"No."

"Excuse me?"

"It is a very bad idea for you to go to a man's house to stay. If a reporter figures it out, then the shit will *really* hit the fan. Think about the headlines—Governor Two-Timed By Miss Snippy."

Marly cringed. "Oh, God."

"Look, I know you don't like it, but you're coming back to Tallahassee with me."

"Yeah, great. I'll take tea with your mom."

"We'll sit down with Lyons, my aide, and Martinez, my campaign manager, and figure out a strategy. We'll draft a statement for the press." Jack's cell phone rang again and he took her by the elbow. "They're outside by now. Do you want to throw a towel over your head?"

It was certainly tempting to just hide…but the reporters already had the awful shots of her and Jack groping each other. Her next appearance needed to be a little more dignified. "No," Marly told him.

"Then hold your head high and smile like you're the queen of England, honey." Jack took a deep breath, asked her if she was ready, and opened the door to chaos.

THE HEADLINES next day were ugly. While Jack stayed closeted with his advisors, Marly stared at the huge black-and-white photograph of them, splashed across the *Miami Herald*, the *Sun Sentinel* and the *Tallahassee Democrat*. Ms. Turlington had helpfully supplied her with several papers and a tray of coffee, along with a bonus disapproving sniff.

In the photos, Marly looked like some voracious vampire vixen, her mouth open, her eyes demonic and her shirt half off.

Jack, oh poor Jack, sported visible wood and his tongue emerged from his mouth toward her. His hair stuck up in a stupid swoop and his eyes were half-closed. He looked like a horny half-wit who wasn't fit to run a hotdog stand, much less the state.

Marly shuddered. The photographs couldn't be worse if imps of Satan had doctored them with a computer program. And as for the headlines...

Jack Cheats On Carol!

Governor 'Gets Some' In The Gables!

Campaigning...Hard?

A call to Alejandro's place had resulted in no answer—the Fabulous Four had probably been rough on him last night. Marly left a message, warning him about the situation outside After Hours and telling him to call her cell phone.

She turned the papers face down and dialed Peggy's cell phone next.

"Peg?"

"Quite the glamour shot, cutie pie."

"So you've seen it. They followed Jack to the salon last night and he didn't notice until all hell broke loose."

"Well, these photographers put the 'rats' in 'paparazzi,' didn't they? And now Shirlie has all the information she ever wanted about the governor's measurements."

Marly groaned. "I should have broken up with him

a week ago. This was a foregone conclusion. Look, I don't really want to talk about it. I just wanted to warn you guys if you hadn't seen it, and let you know that After Hours is probably still surrounded by news crews. They'll try to pump you for information. Just be a doll and tell them 'no comment' until we figure out what to do. Jack is sending over a couple of retired cops to help with any traffic problems you might have."

"Okay. Does Alejandro know?"

"I left a message, but I doubt he's awake yet. He tried to drive the Fab Four home, but they wanted to go to South Beach instead. And if they all ended up at the Living Room or Bed, he's wishing he had a replacement head right now."

"God. Troy just got home last night. I'm going to drag him to the spa with me. He's got more experience handling media than I do, and he'll keep me from getting trampled. I take it you're not coming in today?"

"No. I'm holing up in Tallahassee. Get Shirlie to cancel my appointments, reschedule them for next week if possible."

"Okay, hon. If you need a place to stay when you come back to town, let me know."

"Thanks, Peg. You're a good friend."

"And next time you decide to have a little fun at After Hours, pull the curtains closed!"

Marly sighed. "Yeah."

"Hang in there and look on the bright side—any other photos they have of you guys can't be worse, right?"

Marly laughed weakly and flipped her phone closed. She curled into a ball on Jack's big mahogany bed, shut her eyes and wished she could block out the world. But the world didn't want to be ignored and insisted on shooting images into her brain.

Like, for example, her parents' shocked faces. They'd be humiliated that their daughter was all over the papers, especially since she'd been caught in such a compromising position, looking like a slut on a stick.

She had to call them, but she didn't know what to say. What if her mother answered the phone? Or would it be worse if Dad did? He'd always been so proud of her...until today, when she'd brought him nothing but shame.

Suddenly she sat up, hand to her mouth. What if the media was on their doorstep, too? Investigative reporters were ruthless, and on a story like this they'd leave no stone unturned to dig up more information on her.

Quickly she punched in her parents' number. They had no experience dealing with the media. Her dad would be polite and try to answer their questions, and Ma would make a pot of coffee and some cinnamon buns for the vultures, secretly enjoying the show.

Their number was busy. Oh, God. Were they even now telling the CBS affiliate how hard it had been to potty train her? Sharing her thumb-sucking adventures with NBC? Showing CNN and ABC her prom pictures? And what if the reporters were subtly ridiculing Dad and Ma? They needed help.

Marly began to hyperventilate. She ran to the door and out of Jack's room, down the hall to the huge curving staircase. She hadn't showered yet, and still wore the oversize T-shirt and boxers he'd given her to sleep in. She finger-combed her hair on the way down the stairs and followed the sound of voices.

"Jack!" she called. She arrived at a big set of double doors, wrenched them open and barged in.

Six pairs of eyes under raised brows turned her way. Jack was in the room, but so were his mother, his father—whom she recognized from photographs—two sour-looking men and a woman in a baby-blue suit and pearls.

Mortified, Marly backed out again, leaving nothing but her head craning around the door. "Jack, I can't reach my parents, and I think reporters may have them under siege!"

He came to the door. "They don't know anything about us, do they?"

She shook her head.

"Then don't worry too much about it. I'll send someone over there."

Marly took a deep breath. "Jack, I'm sorry but that's not acceptable. I need to go home—they deserve an explanation from me."

Jack's mouth tightened like a rope around a sack. A sack she was trapped in, struggling. "Stay here with me, Marly. Help me get through this."

She looked beyond him, at the group of family and assistants behind him. He had several people to get him through this. Her parents had nobody but her.

He had a big mansion with electric gates to keep away the media. He had bodyguards and lots of other resources. Her parents had nothing but the dolphin mailbox and the tacky wreath studded with plastic flamingos and gators.

He had handlers to advise him on what to say and staff to answer the door and phone if the reporters got too obnoxious. Her parents didn't.

"Jack, this is non-negotiable. You brought me here and got me into this mess. Now help me get to my parents, if you care about me at all."

18

THE GULFSTREAM LANDED two hours later at Southwest Florida International Airport. Marly loosened her death grip on the arm of the sofa, unfastened her seat belt and climbed out with pilot Alan's help. She'd had no comfort martini this time; she'd just spent the time in the air praying and ignoring the bland PR professional Jack had sent along with her.

She wished for Mike's comforting presence and his scrapbooking to divert her thoughts during the ride to the house, but he was back in Tallahassee and a stranger drove them. Mike traveled with the governor, not with her.

The PR professional, a skinny, nondescript man, tried to feed her appropriate sound bites, but all she registered was his lips moving.

The scene at her parents' house justified her worst fears. They couldn't even pull into the driveway, it was so jammed with cars. A reporter with Channel 7 was in the process of giving live feed and ran over to Marly, microphone extended, as she got out of the limo. "The timing just couldn't be better, folks, because here's the governor's girlfriend right now, arriving home to see Mom and Dad! Ms. Fine, would you care to comment on the recent newspaper headlines?"

The PR guy had warned her not to comment until Jack's office got an official statement together. He put his arm around her and pushed past the hordes, helping Marly get to the front door. "Ms. Fine's first priority is the well-being of her parents. She'll comment later. Thank you. Excuse us. Thank you. Please move aside and remember that you are trespassing on private property. We do hope it won't be necessary to contact local authorities? Thank you. This way, Ms. Fine."

They finally got to the door and Marly came face to face again with the hated wreath of plastic pink flamingos and gators. She rang the bell and yelled, "Dad? Ma! It's me. Will you let me in? Dad!"

A long few moments went by and Marly feared that they were so disgusted with her they planned to leave her outside. But finally the door opened six inches and Dad's face appeared, half-obscured by the Dolphins' cap pulled down to his nose. His hand stretched out to take hers and he yanked her inside.

"Thank you," she mouthed to the PR guy. He nodded and the tide of vultures swept him back off the porch. The limo would take him to a nearby motel, where undoubtedly he'd be pestered all night by reporters who tailed him over there.

Dad pushed away a few microphones and demonstrated to one woman that he really would close her wrist in the door if she didn't remove it. He slammed the bolt home, leaned against it and shook his head. "You know, honey, I didn't like that punk drummer you was with a couple years back. But when I told you to find a better man, I didn't mean Jack Hammersmith!"

Marly gave him a big bear hug. "I'm so sorry, Dad. I can explain everything."

Ma emerged from the kitchen, a dish towel over her shoulder and a cigarette in her mouth. "Marlena, nice of you to join us. Go wash your hands—I been keeping the ham warm for two hours, now."

Uh-oh. Marly kissed her cheek and tried not to think about what she always served with ham: stewed okra and plain boiled potatoes. "Hi, Ma. I like that lipstick you have on. What color is it?"

"Ha. B'lieve it's called Misguided Mauve," Ma said around her cigarette. "Picked it up at the drugstore along with a red called VaVoom Vixen. That one'd look nice on *you.*"

Was that a trace of a smirk at the corner of her mother's mouth? Marly sighed inwardly. Well, what had she expected?

"R'member, use the liquid soap—and not the show towels."

"Yes, ma'am." She walked down the hallway and tossed her overnight bag into the guest room. Her pal Fuzzy was there, no surprise, sprawled belly-up in a puddle of sunshine. He yawned and stretched, spreading his back toes comically apart. Then he twisted his head, saw it was her and hissed.

"You'd look really good purple," she told him, and headed for the bathroom. The green alligator candle with the party hat grinned at her as she soaped her hands and tried to think of what to say to her parents. This wasn't going to be a pleasant conversation.

The governor's hands were up my shirt because I was making a campaign contribution.

Um, my mouth was open in that photo because I was making a heartfelt speech on the part of Democrats all over Florida.

Hammersmith was just sticking his tongue out at me because he didn't agree with my politics. Really.

Somehow, she didn't think they would buy any of this.

She went into the dining room to find Dad warming up the electric carving knife. It sounded, as usual, like a small buzz saw.

Ma staggered in with a ham that could feed twice the number of reporters outside, and dropped it on the two trivets that stood waiting in the center of the table. Then she went back for the okra and boiled potatoes.

Marly looked at it all, tried not to shudder and sat down, putting the pea-green napkin from her placemat into her lap. She aimed a bright smile at her parents.

Dad, anticipating the difficulties to come, had gone ahead and put a bottle of chilled rosé on the table, along with some thick glass goblets. The Precious Moments salt and pepper shakers peeped around the wine bottle, looking as if they'd like some, too.

Ma put out her cigarette in an ashtray on a side table,

then sat down and whipped her own pea-green napkin into her lap. "Look how tender that ham is, Herman." She sounded proud.

"Compliments to the chef," said Marly. She'd seen the Honey-Baked Ham wrapper in the kitchen garbage can.

"Why, thank you." Ma helped herself to some wine and then slid the bottle over to her daughter. "So. You been cutting the governor's hair, have you?"

Marly filled her glass to the rim and inhaled half the contents. "Um, yeah." Through the drawn mustard curtains, she could still see the shapes of heads, shoulders, cars and cameras. *And he says he wants to marry me, but there's not a chance in hell that I can live this way. How does anyone stand it?*

"Nice photos in the paper."

"You liked those, huh? Well, I came over here because I was afraid of this—" she gestured toward the window "—and I thought you might need an explanation and some help."

"Well, now." Ma took a swallow of her wine. "An explanation sure would be nice. But—" she looked at her Timex watch "—help ain't necessary. Sprinklers'll be comin' on in about two minutes, won't they, Herman?"

Dad grinned and set the electric knife down. "They sure will."

Marly put a hand to her mouth. "Did you warn them?"

"Did they warn us?" Ma passed her the bowl of savagely processed okra. "Besides, I gave 'em a statement three hours ago, and they still didn't go away."

Marly dropped the okra. "You *what?*"

"I took 'em out some corn muffins and coffee and talked to 'em."

Oh, God. "What—what did you say?"

"Herman, go switch on the television set so we can watch the six o'clock news. You figure they had time to get it on there?"

He nodded. "I reckon they did." Dad got up and crossed into the formal living room—an open divider delineated the rooms. Amazing that the old Zenith television in the wooden cabinet still functioned, but it did. With a minimum of white noise, Channel Six came on.

"You gave the interview to Six? Not Seven?"

"That little gal with Seven was snotty to me. I showed her. Gave Six the exclusive," said Ma, patting her hair.

Marly set the okra next to Dad's plate, because there was no way she could choke any down right now.

"And coming up next, Six at Six covers the top breaking news story—the Governor's Secret Girlfriend! Six brings you a live interview with Marly Fine's mother and the inside scoop."

Marly's stomach felt as though someone was tossing it up in the air and spinning it like pizza dough. "Scoop?"

Ma inspected her Misguided Mauve matching nail polish and then nodded. "Just watch."

Marly suffered through various commercials for snack foods, new cars and toilet wands before the news came back on. A buxom brunette with too much eye makeup and a Miss Piggy nose announced that she, Roshana Rifkin, was live in Fort Myers with Ms. Fine's mother. She stuck a big black microphone under Ma's small nose.

"Mrs. Fine, what was your reaction when you saw those pictures in the paper this morning? Did you know your daughter was, er, dating the governor?"

Ma turned a blinding smile on the camera and somehow channeled Debbie Reynolds. "Oh, those tabloid journalists. My daughter is such a beautiful girl that I didn't think it was possible to make her look like that. But if they can produce photos of Bigfoot and little green aliens, I guess they can manage an unattractive shot of Marly. Would you like to see a better one?" And she held out Marly's high school graduation picture, in which she looked angelic and sweet, her big blue eyes shown to advantage. The camera swooped in for a close-up.

"Did I tell you how Marly saved her father's life by making him see a special doctor?"

"Er, that's lovely and touching, Mrs. Fine. We'll come back to that. But you don't deny that was your daughter in a compromising position with Governor Hammersmith, do you?"

"Roshana, that…journalist—" she pronounced the word as if it were a cockroach "—caught them off guard, but surely you have to question some of the details? I mean, my daughter is a professional. She'd never let his hair look like that!

"And," her voice dropped to just above a whisper,

"other things have obviously been, well, enhanced. I mean, only a professional basketball player is hung like *that*."

Marly spit her wine all over her lap, while the camera zoomed in on Ms. Rifkin's avid expression.

"So, Mrs. Fine, you're saying the photos have been doctored?"

"Roshana, all I'm suggesting is that the public might want to think about it before they rush to conclusions. Jack is a nice boy, my daughter is a nice girl. The relationship between them is serious—at least on her part. I can tell you that for sure."

Oh, Ma. You're defending me…. Marly's eyes filled with tears and a lump formed in her throat. A lump the size of a limo.

"Here, would you like a corn muffin, Roshana? I baked them special for you nice people, since you've been camped on my lawn all night. I figured you might be hungry." Ma smiled into the camera again.

"Uh, no thanks, Mrs. Fine. So, are you saying that Jack Hammersmith has taken advantage of your daughter?"

"Well, gracious me. I certainly am not a mind reader, dear. You might want to ask him that."

"What about the rumors about him becoming engaged to Carol Hilliard? Don't you think she'll be upset?"

"Who? Sorry, dear, my hearing aid is acting up again." Ma put a hand to her ear. "Oh, gotta run. I have a ham in the oven—you know how it is, Roshana."

"Thank you so much for your time, Mrs. Fine. This

is Roshana Rifkin, reporting live from Fort Myers for Six at Six—your source for the news of the hour."

Marly didn't know whether to laugh or to cry. Ma was an original, if nothing else. She'd hung Jack out to dry in the nicest possible way, but succeeded in defending her daughter. Marly still couldn't believe it. She swallowed the lump and dashed her tears away with the back of her hand. She got up and walked over to Ma. "Thank you," she said, and dropped a kiss on her forehead.

"Aw—it was nothing. That Miss Piggy thought she was all that, didn't she?" Ma patted Marly's back. "That should teach 'em to try to say bad things about my flesh and blood."

So the woman really had given birth to her. She'd wondered sometimes....

"I looked pretty good, don't you think, Marlena? You're right, that Misguided Mauve works real well with the silver-blond color rinse. And, Herman, they say the camera adds ten pounds, but I didn't look too fat, did I?"

"You looked good, Betty Jo. You're a damn Fine woman." He chuckled at the ancient joke, and she dimpled, smacking him in the arm.

"Think you're clever, don't you, old man?"

"I do," he said. "Married you, didn't I?"

Ma giggled like a girl and poured herself some more wine, while Marly wondered what planet they were all on.

In the kitchen, she heard the scrabbling of claws on

the laminate counter, a strangled yowl and a thump. She got up and stuck her head in to find Fuzzy, glaring at her and swishing his tail back and forth.

The plastic butter dish lay overturned on the floor next to him, and he was shaking his left front paw in disgust.

"Landed in the margarine, did you, Fuzz?" She grinned. "Serves you right for hopping up there."

He hissed at her and then licked at his paw.

"Tell you what, dude. We'll make a deal. I'll bring you a piece of ham, but you aren't eating it on my bed."

"Young lady," called Ma's voice. "Now, don't you think you've got some 'splainin' to do?"

19

JACK SAT EXHAUSTED and under siege himself, wondering how Marly was faring in Fort Myers. His public image was taking a serious beating, and Ms. Turlington had been tireless in her pursuit of him with some sort of protein/vitamin shake, which even her crocodile tears couldn't make him drink.

In between bourbons, his father tossed out words like "irresponsible" and "outrageous" and "just plain stupid." Finally, Jack started pouring him doubles to shut him up.

His mother was the only one who asked about Marly. She and Martinez used words like "damage control" and "recovery strategy." Lyons and his PR man pontificated about planting stories with the press and "limited exclusives."

Finally, Jack had had enough. "All of this is beside the point because—"

An aide came hurtling through the double doors with a videotape. "You *will* want to see this, sirs and madam. Right away."

They turned on the plasma television in the room and

loaded the tape. They watched it in silence, all the way to the end. "This is Roshana Rifkin, reporting live from Fort Myers for Six at Six—your source for the news of the hour."

"Jayzus Christ!" Jack's father growled from his leather wing chair. "You dug the grave, but this hillbilly woman's pushed you in and shoveled dirt over the body!"

"Hillbilly?" Senior was talking about his future mother-in-law. "She seems like a nice enough woman. She's just defending her daughter."

"Oh, come on! You can't get involved with a family like that. Get a grip, Jack."

"With a family like what? Didn't you tell me that your great-grandfather was a boot-black?"

Senior succumbed to a coughing fit and crawled back into his bourbon.

His mother rolled her eyes. But she said, "You need to call Carol, Jack. You do owe her an explanation."

"Not only should you call her," Martinez advised, "you should be seen on a very high profile, romantic date with her. At a five-star restaurant. I'll leak it to the press, and you'd better go shopping for a ring right away."

"Whoa, whoa, whoa." Jack blinked rapidly at him. "You know, Martinez, I value your advice on my professional life. But I never asked for it regarding my personal life."

"Excuse me for pointing this out, sir, but right now your professional and personal lives are one and the same."

"Well, we need to change that, then, don't we?"

"I'm not sure it's possible, sir."

Jack walked over to the man and glared down at him. "Martinez, I have given up years of my life for Florida politics and for this family, but I draw the line at marrying the wrong woman for them. But let's say I was willing to do that. You think it would be *damage control* to give Carol an engagement ring now?"

"Yes, sir, I do."

Well, then all that hair spray has gotten to your brain. "You're crazy. If I did that, the media shit-storm would double, because it would appear to validate that I'd been cheating on Carol! And it would also make Marly look like some two-bit piece of tail I was messing around with."

Martinez's bland, calculating look said it all. Jack wanted to hit him, knock him sprawling on his ass. But he restrained himself.

"Which she is *not.* I intend to marry her. Understand, Martinez? So why don't you guys figure how to spin *that.*"

Martinez exchanged an aghast look with Lyons.

"Jesus, Jack!" His father struggled up out of his wing chair, sloshing bourbon onto his knee. "You can't throw away your political future by getting hitched to a hairdresser."

"John!" said Mrs. Hammersmith.

"Watch yourself, Senator," Jack warned. "I think you're afraid I'm throwing away your own vicarious thrills. My life is not a spectator sport for your amusement—or anyone else's."

"Excuse me." Lyons had been quiet during most of the verbal brawl, but now he spoke up. "Jack, we…didn't know you felt this way. We just assumed, er, that you weren't serious about the girl."

Jack leveled an ominous gaze on his aide. "Well, I am."

Lyons squirmed. "Uh, yes, sir. But we already sent a statement to the associated press, along with a photo of you and Carol. The one from her birthday party."

"You *what?*" Jack's jaw worked. "Exactly who the hell is 'we'? And when is press time?"

"Press time's not relevant in this case, I'm afraid. The information's probably been uploaded to the Internet."

Jack rushed him, fists clenched, and the poor guy squeaked, ducking his head. "Who is *we?*" Jack thundered.

"M-me, M-Martinez and S-S-Senator Ha—"

"You're fired. All of you."

His dad roared, "You need Hilliard's campaign contribution, boy! And you can't fire me—I'm your father."

"Wanna bet?" Jack stalked out of the room to call Marly and then Carol and straighten out this ungodly mess.

JACK BEGS FORGIVENESS! *Rumor Has It That The Governor Is Shopping For A Ring.*

Marly stared at the image on her father's desktop computer screen, unable to process what it was telling her. Jack grinned back at her, his arm around Carol Hilliard's waist in an expression of casual intimacy. The woman was breathtaking, groomed to within an inch of her life, looking like a life-size, lickable, chocolate-covered fashion doll.

Marly wished that she could pop Carol's head off and watch it roll across the floor. She wished she could toss it into Fuzzy's food bowl or even into the toilet.

But Jack…she didn't know what was bad enough to do to that treacherous, lying son of a bitch. Because the date on the photograph was barely more than a week ago! Right after she'd seen him, and he'd spouted a lot of promises and reassurances and announcements about how she was The One.

She was The One, all right. The One stupid enough to start to believe him. The One who'd guarded a secret hope that he was telling the truth. The One who'd protested his macho assumption that she'd just let herself be swept down the aisle—but covertly admired his cock-sureness.

She'd asked him to send her home to her parents, and he'd quickly done it…probably with a huge sense of relief. It got her out of the way, of course, while he figured out how to salvage his political future. She'd been an idiot.

Now he'd probably call and blame the AP photo and statement somehow on his handlers, his PR team. He'd claim no knowledge of their actions and beg—but not too hard—for her forgiveness. And when she told him where to go, he'd accept it on the surface with sad grace, while internally whooping that he was off the hook.

Then would come the television interview with a devoted Carol, in front of the entire state. He would apologize to her and the people, claiming that he'd had a last moment of bachelor panic before asking her to be his wife. The people would understand and applaud his honesty. They'd admire Carol for standing by her man. And they'd elect the charismatic Jack for a second term...because he was so human, underneath his fairy-tale existence. Ugh!

Marly shot back from the computer and ran into the guest bathroom, where she promptly threw up. Then, without thinking, she washed her face with her mother's orange and pineapple soaps and dried it with the *show* towels.

She fled from there into the guest room and curled up in the center of the bed, dried-eyed but aching. She lay in a fetal position, next to Fuzzy, who looked at her warily but didn't hiss—to her amazement. Fuzzy had been in the process of licking his nether regions, and he continued with that, keeping one eye on her.

"Why?" she whispered to the cat. "Why did he have to see my photo? Why did he lie? Why did he use me like that?"

Fuzzy twitched an ear and spat some hair off his small tongue.

"There are a million other girls in Florida. Beach bodies, supermodels, exotic babes. Why me?"

The cat swiped a paw over his nose and twitched his tail.

"Why?" she whispered again. "And oh, God. Why was I stupid enough to let him get past my defenses? Why did I have to go and fall in love with him?"

Fuzzy blinked. Then, as if he could sense her distress, he licked her arm soothingly.

Marly went ahead and let the tears flow. "I never knew you could be nice," she sobbed. "Nobody is what they seem these days."

It was about half an hour later that the phone began to ring again, and with her parents' okay, she unplugged it completely. She didn't want to talk to reporters, Jack or his handlers. They could all take a flying leap.

She shut off her cell phone and the lights in her room and just lay there in the dark with Fuzzy. They had a new understanding: if she didn't roll on him, then he wouldn't bite her. Their relationship had come a long way because of the ham.

JACK FLEW TO MIAMI immediately. On his way to Carol's courtesy of Mike, he cursed for the thirtieth time and clicked his cell phone shut.

There were two possibilities for why Marly and her parents weren't answering the phone. One, they were dodging reporters. Two, they'd seen the photo and Internet headlines and were dodging *him*.

He supposed she could have come back to Miami by now, flying a regular carrier. He didn't know, and it was driving him crazy.

Jack soon faced Carol and a sea of French Provincial furniture in her Coral Gables condo. She looked cool and calm as always, as poised as a model.

"It's not you, it's me," he said. "You're a very special girl, Carol, but I don't think I can give you what you want. I can't give you my heart. I love you dearly as a friend, but I'm not *in* love with you."

"Do me a favor, darling. Spare me the canned lines, all right?"

He looked away from her steady, brown-eyed gaze. "I'm sorry. I guess I just don't know what to say. I wish I could be in love with you, Carol. You're perfect in every way…except that you're like a sister to me."

"Well, I'm guessing that you're like a brother to me, after all, because I'm really not devastated. But I do have an overpowering urge to lower your bare butt into a pit of snapping turtles!"

Startled, Jack laughed.

"What in the hell were you *thinking* when you allowed your people to send that photo to the press?"

"I wasn't!"

"That's for sure."

"I mean, I didn't allow them. They just did it—after talking with my father. When I found out, I fired them, but the damage is done."

Irritation crossed her lovely face. "Your father and my father. Those two old coots should get married. They're impossible. The only reason I was going along with the whole thing is that I haven't found anyone better than you, Jack."

He winced. "Thank you…I think. But you will.

There is a man out there who will make your toes curl. And it's not me. I know that."

She flushed. "Well, what do you want to do to clear up the misunderstanding?"

He told her. "I think we need to give a press conference, Carol. You and me, nobody else. And the word has to come from you. *You* are not in love with *me*. You know everyone thinks we make a cute couple, but it's not in the cards because I'm like a brother to you. That way I don't look like a heel for 'dumping' you or 'cheating' on you, and you look like a goddess, gorgeous and confident enough to turn down Jack Hammersmith. You'll probably have sheikhs and princes calling you after this interview airs."

"Actually—" she stuck her chin out "—I already do."

It was the first visible sign that he'd hurt her feelings, and he felt like a jerk. "Jeez, Carol. I'm impressed."

To his relief, she went back to being the ten-year-old girl he'd buried in the sand and dunked in the ocean. "Don't be. The sheikh in question is short and bald and already has three wives."

Jack grinned. "And I'm betting your father doesn't want camels or sheep grazing his polo fields?"

"Correct. You were the more attractive option. But as I told him, I don't need to be married to the governor. I think I'll have a president instead."

"You'd have no problem, Carol," he said, and meant it.

She smiled. "I know."

JACK'S NEXT STOP was at After Hours, just in case Marly was there. Mike pulled the limo up outside the spa, and Jack straightened his tie, took a deep breath and walked in. "Is Marly here?" he asked Shirlie.

She eyed him as if he were a cockroach, every blond curl on her head vibrating with hostility. "If she were, I don't know why I'd tell *you*."

Ouch.

Shirlie snapped her gum. "Even if you are hung like a bull—"

Jack choked.

"—which I'm not saying you are, because the camera does add ten pounds, right? Anyway, it's not worth it. She doesn't need a pig like you in her life."

The bleached-blond guy—what was his name, Nicky?—skipped up from his abandoned client, put his hands on his hips and looked Jack over from head to toe in a disgusted way. "Governor," he declared, "you are a *slut.*"

"Hey! Can you guys give me a chance to explain? I need to talk to Marly."

"Explain what? How you can't keep your zipper up? Sweetie, if you were gay…"

Jack blanched at the thought.

"If you were gay, I wouldn't do you with somebody *else's* equipment. Not even if you wore black leather chaps, which are the biggest turn-on in the world. *That* is how low you are."

"Are you finished?" Jack asked.

"No. I wouldn't put you out on the curb with the

recycling." And Nicky stamped his foot, spun around and marched away. "*Now* I'm finished!" he called over his shoulder.

Jesus Christ. Nobody in this place was going to help him, that much was obvious. "Marly!" Jack yelled at the top of his lungs. "Marly, you have to listen to me!"

A little red-headed vixen in a white lab coat came out from the back, next. Arms folded across her chest, she glared at him. "You know, Governor, I was a place kicker for my college football team. How'd you like me to make a field goal with your testicles?"

Jack gaped at her. "You know what? You people are crazy. I haven't done anything wrong. My aides sent out the photo and statement without consulting me." He looked beyond her at a big, strapping Latino guy who was headed his way. Uh-oh. Jack locked his knees and curled his hands into loose fists.

"May I help you, sir?" asked the man, aiming a cold, black-eyed stare in his direction.

"I need to see Marly. Is she here?"

"No. Can I give her a message for you, Governor?" There was just a trace of menace in the guy's voice.

"Do you know where she is?"

"I do not. I do know that she doesn't want any contact with you, however. So let me show you to the door."

The damned door was in plain sight right behind him, so Jack took this as a veiled offer to toss him out on his gubernatorial ass.

"You're Alejandro, right?"

The guy nodded.

"And you're Peggy." He addressed the little redhead. She just narrowed her eyes on him.

"Look, just tell her...tell her to watch the news tonight, okay? It's very important."

Jack looked at each hostile face and wondered if they'd get the message to her. He hoped so. Then he turned and walked out the door.

20

AT APPROXIMATELY 5:55 p.m., a polite knocking commenced on Dad and Ma's door in Fort Myers. *Oh, no,* Marly thought. *The reporters have started up again.* There were only a few of them left on the street, and they were no longer in the driveway or on the porch, thank God, since Dad had called local law enforcement to threaten them with trespass charges.

She ignored the knocking, and so did her parents. Ma looked up briefly from her soap digest magazine, and Dad grumbled behind the newspaper, but neither made a move toward the door.

But whoever was there wasn't giving up. The knocking became a pounding, and the pounding finally morphed into outright battering.

"Jiminy Christmas!" Dad exclaimed. "If they dent our door, I'll send those vultures a bill." He struggled to get up, but Marly said, "I'll deal with it."

She stalked to the door, not caring if she was covered in cat hairs or had sheet marks on her face. She threw it open, prepared to rip the offending reporter a new butt hole, only to stop and stare. "Miss Turlington?"

The governor's personal assistant stood there, holding up one of her hideous shoes—the object she'd been using to pound on the door. "Miss Fine," she said stiffly, straightening her pearls and manufacturing a tortured smile. She bent, set her loafer down and stuck her suntan-panty-hose-covered foot back into it. "May I come in?"

"Um. Of course." Bemused, Marly opened the screen door and stood aside to let her pass.

The woman looked at her watch, spied the Zenith and hustled across the living room. "Excuse me, but I'm under direct orders from the gov—"

Dad ejected himself from his La-Z-Boy. "I'll have you know, Miss Whos-y-whats, that Jack Hammersmith has no jurisdiction in my living room! Touch my Zenith and I won't be responsible for my actions." He shook the rolled-up newspaper at her.

Ms. T. flattened herself against the television, a martyr till the end. "I'm under direct orders to make sure Miss Fine watches the six o'clock news!" She looked like an aging sacrificial maiden, chained to the rocks and waiting for a dragon to come and devour her.

Marly bit back the giggles that threatened to overwhelm her at the sight. "Dad, calm down. Miss Turlington, step away from the Zenith. I will turn it on. Please tell me that the Jack-Ass didn't fly you here in the Gulfstream to ensure that I witness whatever PR maneuver he's about to pull off?"

"Well, young lady, I wouldn't sound so shocked if

I were you. If you'd only answer your telephone, such drastic and dramatic gestures wouldn't be necessary."

"I'll thank you not to take that tone with my daughter, Miss Turli-Top!" Ma had surged off the sofa and toward their guest. She poked her in her fleshless breastbone, so that Turls backed up to get away from her. "Have a seat." She shoved her into a rigidly uncomfortable side chair.

"That's Turlington, madam."

"Whatever. What channel, did you say?"

"Seven."

"Turn the TV to seven, Herman. Marly, move out of the way so we can all see."

The camera was focused on an empty podium, and a reporter's voice could be heard in the background. "Now, in just a few moments, folks, Jack Hammersmith will be making his first live public statement since the scandal regarding his hairstylist girlfriend broke in Coral Gables a couple of days ago. We have been unable to speak with Marlena Fine, the woman in question."

The camera panned to Jack as he entered the room, looking sober and deeply gubernatorial. His royal-blue tie gleamed softly under the intense TV lighting, contrasting with the snowy-white of his shirt and the dark cloth of his suit. Marly's heart skipped a beat—until the camera showed Carol Hilliard at his side. Then her stomach rose up in revolution and knocked her heart into oblivion.

Oh, God. He was going to formally announce his engagement to that woman, and she was going to vomit all over her parents' shag carpeting and possibly on Miss Turlington's ugly shoes. She staggered toward the back hall. "I can't and won't watch this."

Turls popped out of her seat and caught her by the arm. "You have to watch!" Her bony claw held surprising strength.

"I don't have to do any—"

Jack began to speak in quiet tones as they struggled. "I know that after some surprising and disturbing newspaper headlines, the people of Florida are wondering what's going on in my personal life. I'd like to thank you for your patience and end your speculation today with this press conference. I am here with my childhood companion and friend, Carol Hilliard...."

"Let go of me!" Marly snapped at Miss Turlington.

"Pay attention!" the woman screeched back.

"Get your hands off my daughter!" Dad's voice thundered out.

"Everybody, *shut up!*" yelled Ma.

"The polls have been informing us for a year now that voters think Carol and I are perfect for each other, that we make a great couple, that she's the ultimate Jackie to my JFK."

Marly's stomach heaved again.

"That's nice. But it's idyllic thinking. And it's a fairy tale—let me tell you why. There is, or was, only one JFK, just as there was only one Jackie. Whether or not their marriage was perfect is the subject of a lot of speculation, and I don't have any of the answers. But Carol and I are not going to become a couple just because poll numbers suggest that we should. We're not prepared to live a lie.

"Carol and I will *not* be announcing our engagement today—or ever," Jack's voice continued, "although it's not because of the recent scandal."

Marly froze.

"Carol, as you can see, is a lovely, multitalented and charming lady. She will make some lucky man a wonderful wife one day."

"But it won't be Jack," Carol said, leaning into the microphone and putting her arm around his shoulder. "Because I'm not in love with him. I've known him all my life, and I adore him, but he's like a brother to me." She smiled at him and gave him a squeeze. "I don't want to marry my brother."

Jack spoke again. "As for me, I'm in love with somebody else, and her name is Marly Fine."

"What?" Marly stopped trying to pull away from Miss Turlington and instead leaned on her for support. Her knees wobbled and she finally just sank down onto the shag carpet, folding her legs underneath her.

Jack kept on speaking. "I met Marly only a few weeks ago, but I know that I love her and want her in my life. There are a lot of people who have questioned my judgment on this, and to them I say—if you've trusted me to run the state of Florida, can you not trust my ability to choose a wife? To read my own heart?

"If not, then I believe I should step down right now and not run for reelection, because you sure don't have a lot of confidence in me.

"Since I've been in office, I've been committed to my campaign promises—addressing the falling literacy rates in the state, the immigration issues, better hurricane preparedness and disaster relief efforts for those in need. I have also been committed to Florida families, even as a bachelor governor.

"Now it's time that I be committed to my own heart and to the woman I love. If that's going to damage my political image, then so be it. I wouldn't ask a single one of you to marry for any other reason than love. I hope you won't expect any different of me.

"We all find love unexpectedly, in all kinds of odd places. Some people find love in high school or college. Some find it next door. Others find love on a train, a flight or a whole other continent. I happened to find love in a hair salon. Is that so hard to believe? I wasn't in a bar, with alcohol clouding my judgment. I wasn't a kid in my teens or early twenties. And I wasn't looking for a woman deliberately through some kind of match service or blind date.

"Marly walked into the room, and I didn't care what kind of room it was, or what time of day, or if my political advisors would think it was a good idea. I took one look at her, and I was gone." Jack stopped speaking for a moment and looked down, tightening his hands on the edges of the podium.

"I wish that I could announce my engagement to Marly Fine right now, this minute. But there's one little hitch—I haven't been able to ask her a simple question. So I may as well ask her right now, in front of God and everyone. Marly, will you marry me? It doesn't have to be next week or next month or even next year. We could have the longest engagement of all time. Just say yes. Please."

Miss Turlington dabbed at her eyes with a lace-trimmed handkerchief while Marly stared stupidly at the television screen, at the governor baring his soul in front of the entire state…for *her*.

Jack pulled a small, black-velvet box out of his pocket. "I've got the ring right here."

She gasped, along with the entire audience at the press conference, her parents and Ms. T., who said, "I can assure you that I did *not* choose that for him, like Carol Hilliard's birthday present."

A glow began inside Marly's heart. Jack wasn't a liar. He wasn't a cheap opportunist. He probably was crazy, but he was a good kind of crazy….

"Size six and a half. But I'm not opening this box until I'm in front of you, down on one knee."

Ohmigod. He even knows my ring size. Even though the rat must have gone back to that security file to get it.

"Aw, come on, Jack!" yelled a reporter. "Show us the rock!"

"Yeah! Give us a look!" called another.

He shook his head. "Nope. Sorry, guys. She has the right to see it first."

"Show us the darn ring!" shrieked Ma, bouncing up and down on the sofa. "I wanna see the ring! That *tease*." She shoved the ancient rotary dial phone at

Marly. "Call him, Marlena! Tell him he's killing us, here, already."

"Ma, he's not going to answer his cell phone while he's on live television."

"You don't know that until you try, do you? Call him!"

"And say what?"

Ma stared at her. "What, are you stupid? Say *yes!* And then tell him I want to see the ring. Ohmigod, Herman, wait until my bunko group hears that our daughter is marrying the *governor*...."

Heart in her throat, Marly dialed Jack's cell phone number. Embarrassing to admit she knew it by heart, but she did. Amazed, she watched the television screen as he reached inside his jacket and pulled out the phone. He looked down at the origination number and gave a huge, young-Dennis-Quaid grin. "Excuse me, folks, but I have to take this call. I believe it's from the lady in question."

He flipped open the phone. "Hello?"

"Jack? It's me."

"Hi, honey. You're not calling to break my heart, are you? Anything but that."

"Um, I don't think so. But I was hoping we could talk about this face-to-face? A little less publicly?"

"I understand. Can I pick you up in an hour?"

"Yes."

"Can I tell them there's hope?"

"Yes."

"That's all I need to hear, then. I love you."

"I—" Marly swallowed hard. "I think I love you, too. But I'd make a horrible political wife."

"We'll see about that."

Ma screeched, "The ring! Tell him we want to see the ring!"

Jack said dryly, "Your mom sure sounds excited."

"Yeah, well, I think she can wait an hour to see it. I kind of agree with you that I'd like to see it first. It's a girl thing."

"Being the prospective bride, and all."

"Prospective. Keep that in mind."

"Marly, honey, are you still gonna play hard to get?"

"It's just my nature." But she smiled.

Jack groaned. "Be there before you know it." He flipped his phone closed and stepped back to the podium. "Marly," he informed everyone, "says she's thinking about it."

The crowd went nuts.

21

JACK WAS ACTUALLY nervous as the limo, followed by a Lincoln containing the ever-present Jimmy and Rocket, pulled up to a modest little house with a dolphin mailbox and a door wreath dotted with pink flamingos and green gators. He grinned.

They weren't Marly's style at all and she was probably mortified by them. But then again, wasn't it some kind of law that parents existed to embarrass their children? He figured he'd have his own explaining to do next time the senator closed his tie in an ice bucket after a few too many bourbons. Or pinched Marly's ass.

News vans and reporters lined the narrow street and correspondents converged on the limo, shouting questions and waving microphones and generally making a nuisance of themselves. They weren't camped in the yard, though, probably due to the six yellow tractor sprinklers shooting water everywhere. He grinned. That's one way to handle 'em.

He exchanged a look with Mike, who'd flown with them on the Gulfstream to Fort Myers. Jack had even helped him arrange a couple of pages in the latest scrapbook. He had personally chosen the pink gingham border and the cut-paper tulips that surrounded the photos of Mike's daughter. He'd also served as a consultant on the white picket fence and the smiley-faced sun in the top right-hand corner. Damn, he was good.

Jack pulled off his tie and left it with his jacket in the car. Then he slid out of the limo, shoved his hands into his pockets and made his way up the sidewalk, flanked by Frick and Frack. Despite his security detail, the reporters swarmed around, but he ignored them, other than saying, "Hi, I had a feeling you guys would be here."

"Are you here to propose to Marly?"

"Governor, what do you mean, she's thinking about it?"

Jack reached the flamingo and gator wreath, knocked on the door and begged them all for twenty minutes of privacy. Then he promised he'd make a statement and answer questions.

The door opened about four inches, and an angular old face adorned with a thatch of silvery hair peered out at him. "Good God Amighty, it's really him, Betty Jo!"

"Lemme see! Move out of the way, old man." A woman's face ducked under the man's arm. Wide blue eyes set in deeply tanned skin registered Jack's presence. Her mauve lips opened and she squeaked with excitement.

"Hi, I'm Jack Hammersmith. You must be Mr. and Mrs. Fine. It's a pleasure to make your acquaintance."

Jack stuck out his hand, half-afraid that they might close it in the door. But the man opened it farther, and the woman locked onto the gubernatorial hand and yanked him inside. Jimmy and Rocket remained outside, one in the front and one circling to the back of the house.

"We are right delighted to meet you, Mr. Governor," said Marly's mother. "Please come on in and have a seat."

"Thanks."

"Would you like a glass of iced tea? A corn muffin?"

"No, thank you…"

They tried to install him in what was clearly the king of the castle's La-Z-Boy, but Jack looked up and saw Marly standing there, taking in the scene with amusement. "Hi," she said softly. "I can't believe you're here."

He moved toward her, taking in her bare feet, long sea-foam-green cotton gypsy skirt, and simple white tank top. Around her neck she wore a shell that dangled from a brown leather band. Her eyes shone a deep, clear blue-green and her skin was freshly scrubbed. Her hair was in its regulation braid, which she'd pulled over her left shoulder. He'd never seen anyone so beautiful.

He clenched his hand around the box in his pocket, and her eyes followed the movement. Then she looked meaningfully at her father, and Jack picked up on the clue.

"Mr. Fine, may I speak with you privately for a **moment?**"

"Why, yessir."

He followed the man into his formal dining room, where they had a seat at the table. Marly's mother suddenly discovered something that she urgently had to do in the kitchen, right next to the dining room's open door.

"I've never really, uh, done this before," said Jack. "So I guess I'll get right to the point. I was hoping for your blessing, sir, since I'd like to marry your daughter."

Mr. Fine sneezed twice in quick succession, and so Jack felt obliged to bless *him*. Then he sat hoping for his turn.

"You love her, do you?"

"Yes, sir, I do. I said it right on television."

"You'll treat her right?"

"Always and forever."

"You think I could, uh, borrow her back every once in a while?"

Jack put his hand on the man's shoulder and squeezed. "I think we could probably arrange that." He smiled. "Not that she'll ask my permission about anything."

"No, that she won't." Mr. Fine looked down at his worn, callused hands, seeming to hesitate. Then he said, "She ain't a fancy dinner party kind of gal. Don't go trying to change her, you hear?"

Jack said quietly, "I love her just the way she is. I wouldn't change a thing."

Herman Fine met his gaze squarely and then stuck out his hand. "Well, then, you got my blessing."

MARLY GUESSED she was her mother's daughter, after all, since she wasn't too proud to eavesdrop, either—from behind the other doorway. Tears filled her eyes at her father's words and at Jack's responses. And they continued as Jack shared the story of his great-great-grandfather and the cameo of his Italian bride.

They caught her red-handed when she sniffled and they both stuck their heads around the doorway.

"What?" she said defensively. "Like you wouldn't have done the same thing?"

Her father shook her head at her and disappeared into the kitchen, saying that he and Betty Jo were going to take a run to the grocery store.

Jack grinned and admitted that he'd have had a cup to the wall. "So," he said, sidling up to her and nudging her with his hip, "have you been thinking?"

The hip in question was covered with a pocket, in which there was some kind of box. Marly had a feeling she knew what the box might contain.

"Yes. I've been thinking."

Jack got down on one knee. "Have you been thinking what I'm thinking?"

"Jack, wait."

"Nope, I can't wait anymore. I'm all waited out."

"But I have some questions! Serious questions."

"Okay." He sighed. "Shoot."

"As the governor's wife, could I still wear blue toenail polish?"

"Yep. You'll be a trendsetter."

"And rubber flip-flops?"

"Anywhere but the White House or a formal dinner, babe."

"Can I still disagree with you politically? Because I will, you know."

"I count on you to disagree with me. Life would be boring if you didn't. Just do me a favor and don't call the Republican Party *the Dark Side* in public."

"That's a lot to ask, you know."

"Yeah, I'm a real demanding sonuvabitch. Now can I get on with the proposal?"

"No. I still have questions."

"Jeez," he said. "You sure are hard on a guy's knee-caps!"

"Sorry. But this is important. As the governor's wife, could I still cut hair?"

Jack ruminated. "As long as disgruntled clients can't sue the state government for damages, I think it'd be okay."

"Jack, I've never had a disgruntled client. Well, maybe one. But that was back in beauty school, and her hair didn't stay purple for more than a couple of hours, I promise."

"What a relief… I have a thought, though. You can definitely still cut hair if you want to, but here's the thing—I'm not the poorest guy you've ever dated. So if you want to keep your partnership in the salon but only work a couple of days a week, you have that option. The other few days a week you could either be a devoted gubernatorial wife or you could paint."

"I think I'd paint," she admitted. "Not that I'm saying yes yet or anything."

"Look, my kneecaps are cracking under the weight of my body, here. You either have to agree to marry me, or you have to break up with me for good. I insist."

"Well, I don't want to break up with you," Marly told him. "I've kind of gotten used to you, and if you want to know the truth—" she leaned forward and whispered in his ear "—I'm really horny."

Jack brightened and fished out the black-velvet box. "Marry me, honey, and we can take care of that right away. Your parents are out, and there's a guest room here, right?"

The ring was gorgeous: a two-carat pear. Marly took pity on him and said yes. But when he kissed her and wrestled her tenderly down the hallway to the guest room, it was occupied. Fuzzy stared at them balefully from the center of the bed.

"Oh, boy," Marly said. "This is going to take a lot of ham."

If you enjoyed what you just read,
then we've got an offer you can't resist!

Take 2 bestselling
love stories FREE!
Plus get a FREE surprise gift!

Clip this page and mail it to Harlequin Reader Service®

IN U.S.A.	IN CANADA
3010 Walden Ave.	P.O. Box 609
P.O. Box 1867	Fort Erie, Ontario
Buffalo, N.Y. 14240-1867	L2A 5X3

YES! Please send me 2 free Harlequin® Blaze™ novels and my free surprise gift. After receiving them, if I don't wish to receive anymore, I can return the shipping statement marked cancel. If I don't cancel, I will receive 6 brand-new novels each month, before they're available in stores! In the U.S.A., bill me at the bargain price of $3.99 plus 25¢ shipping and handling per book and applicable sales tax, if any*. In Canada, bill me at the bargain price of $4.47 plus 25¢ shipping and handling per book and applicable taxes**. That's the complete price and a savings of at least 10% off the cover prices—what a great deal! I understand that accepting the 2 free books and gift places me under no obligation ever to buy any books. I can always return a shipment and cancel at any time. Even if I never buy another book from Harlequin, the 2 free books and gift are mine to keep forever.

151 HDN D7ZZ
351 HDN D72D

Name	(PLEASE PRINT)	
Address	Apt.#	
City	State/Prov.	Zip/Postal Code

Not valid to current Harlequin® Blaze™ subscribers.

Want to try two free books from another series?
Call 1-800-873-8635 or visit www.morefreebooks.com.

* Terms and prices subject to change without notice. Sales tax applicable in N.Y.
** Canadian residents will be charged applicable provincial taxes and GST.
  All orders subject to approval. Offer limited to one per household.
  ® and ™ are registered trademarks owned and used by the trademark owner and/or its licensee.

BLZ05   ©2005 Harlequin Enterprises Limited.